UNTHINKABLE

Rory McGouran

First published 2024
by Rowanvale Books Ltd
The Gate
Keppoch Street
Roath
Cardiff
CF24 3JW
www.rowanvalebooks.com

A CIP catalogue record for this book is available from the British Library.
Paperback ISBN: 978-1-83584-077-1
eBook ISBN: 978-1-83584-060-3

For Val, my wife, who has tolerated years of enthusiasms and procrastinations in the writing of this book.

CONTENTS

PART ONE:

NOVEMBER 1995

CHAPTER ONE

The returning tide had reached the wreck of the *Jura*. The North Sea was calm and the water came in rivulets which flowed quickly along gullies and wrinkles in the sand, coalescing and silently flooding the beach. A gull circled the wreck, where a man sat with his back against a rusting strut, severely hypothermic, past shivering and almost past caring, until the feel of the icy water on his feet and calves jerked him back towards consciousness and the realisation of where he was. He was sitting on the sand with his feet out in front of him, right arm extended above, and already his legs were underwater. He turned to his right, pulling his knees up beneath him, and felt with his left hand for something to grip. He found a handhold in the metal, and then he was standing facing the remains of the wreck, his right wrist handcuffed to a rail at waist level.

It was pitch dark, a moonless November night. The sand dunes were four hundred yards away but he could see nothing and his panicked shouts vanished into the darkness, unheard.

The big spring tide came in quickly, and within minutes the water was knee deep. He tugged hard against the metal of the cuffs, ripping the flesh of his wrist, but his hand was held tight. Soon the water reached his waist. He struggled to stay upright against the pull of the tide as the sea crept up his body, but he was floated off his feet. He managed to twist himself so he lay on his back, anchored by the handcuffs. His face was slapped by wavelets and he tried to hold his breath, but the sea washed into his nose, making him cough, and he could no longer control his breathing. He felt a crushing pain in his chest as his panicked gasps filled his lungs with seawater, drowning him, and he thrashed about in terror, slapping the water with his free hand.

The bad bit was over soon, however, and then he was peaceful, floating oblivious below the surface, until the writhing and jerking of his body stopped and his mind shut down for ever.

***

Four o'clock on a Saturday afternoon in November with rugby on the telly was not the time to be on Massingham Beach, so thought Senior Coastguard George Peters, hunched over the wheel of the truck as he drove across the sand. He had been a coastguard for over twenty years and knew this stretch of the coast as well as anyone. Drownings were not uncommon, sometimes two or three a year. The beaches were flat and the tide went out a long way, often as much as a quarter of a mile, exposing vast expanses of sand. When it returned it came fast, cutting off segments of beach which would soon be several feet underwater. Last year a ten-year-old child had drowned, lost when her parents' attention was briefly elsewhere. Like most bodies, she washed ashore a few weeks later, thirty miles to the east where the current had taken her. He had never known a body to wash up on Massingham Beach.

He glanced across at his colleague. "You tell your birdwatcher that if this is a wild goose chase, I'm going to get his telescope and stuff it—"

"Yes, of course," Michael said. "I'll tell him. I expect he'll be pleased you've decided against his binoculars. But come on, George, we've been told there's a body tangled in the wreck—we can't just ignore it!"

"Go over it again."

"He was birdwatching on the beach at dawn. The tide was right out. He saw some waders close to the wreck and walked towards them but they flew away. By then he was a bit beyond the wreck and realised the tide was coming in. He knows this coast and was aware of the danger, so he turned to go back. That's when he saw what he thought was a bundle of clothes, but when he got nearer he could see it was a body. He only had time for a quick look, the tide was almost at the wreck, but he's certain it was a body."

"Well, here's the wreck, so we'll know soon enough. Remember the story?"

"Practice for the bombers?"

"She was a bunkering ship when the Second World War began, overdue for the knacker's yard. She was going to be sunk in the harbour mouth of Lowestoft if the Germans showed signs of invading the east coast. When this threat was over, she was towed around to Massingham Beach and the bombers flying from Norfolk airfields used her as target practice. No complaints from the locals of course; free coal on the beach."

He stopped the Toyota. Not much of the *Jura* was left visible now, just some chunks of rusting superstructure, a few vertical spars and segments of railing. They got out, walking carefully, watching the corrugated sand, avoiding the puddles, which could be deeper than their boots. The air was dank, fishy and salty, and they could hear the waves of the low tide away to their left. There was little breeze but it was bitterly cold.

The body lay on its side on the sand, right wrist still handcuffed, twisted awkwardly where the man's shoulder had dislocated in the strong tide. George swore quietly when he saw the swollen, battered face. He called the police station in Market Houghton and drove back to the car park in the dunes to collect Detective Sergeant Hicks, leaving Michael with the body.

Hicks came straight from Market Houghton in a squad car, blue light flashing. The coast road was quiet at this time of year, and he arrived in the car park not long after George. He was short with black hair, a pale face with a five o'clock shadow, and a pronounced Norfolk accent. The knees and elbows of his navy suit were shiny and his black shoes were scuffed. George, in contrast, was tall, heavily built with thick, curly brown hair and a weather-beaten face, imposing in his uniform.

"We've got an hour at the most before the tide's back," he told Hicks.

"I hope you've touched nothing," Hicks said over his shoulder, collecting his bag from the squad car.

"You won't get much. He's been underwater for twelve hours at least."

When they reached the *Jura*, Hicks took a camera from his bag and photographed the body from several angles. He pulled on gloves and carefully examined the handcuffs. "How are we going to free him?"

"We've got cutters in the van."

Hicks' phone rang. A colleague had arrived in the car park with the body bag, and Michael drove back in the truck to collect it.

Hicks watched anxiously. "What do we do if the truck gets stuck in the sand?"

"I don't have a Plan B to deal with that," George confessed. "Actually, when I come to think of it, I don't have a Plan A either. We should cut him free now. The sea's nearly here."

"Great," Hicks muttered. He was beginning to shiver in the cold. In the rush to get to the wreck before the tide, he had left his coat in the station. He had stood in several puddles, and his shoes and lower trousers were soaked.

He looked around again: sand, shells, seaweed, rusted struts and a handcuffed body. Nothing else. He took a number of photos and then walked slowly around the wreck. The structure was rusty and corroded with cracks and crevices in the metal. He peered into the accessible ones and, when he couldn't see inside, felt nervously with his fingers. He was about six feet from where Michael was starting to cut the body free when he noticed a large hole in one of the struts where the metal had corroded away, big enough to take his hand, and he felt gingerly inside.

"There might be a crab in that one" George warned.

There was sand in the bottom of the hole. Hicks felt a small piece of metal, which he pulled out and showed to the coastguard, who shrugged. "No idea. Looks like a key of some sort."

"Could be a handcuffs key," Hicks said. He tried it, and the cuffs opened easily.

CHAPTER TWO

Angus Wilson, pathologist at St Paul's, arrived at the hospital at 8.30. He had his own parking slot for which, to his great satisfaction, he paid nothing, having somehow escaped the attention of hospital managers who tended to avoid the mortuary. He noticed the police car parked on the grass beside a large No Parking sign.

Hicks and Tracey, the mortuary attendant, were drinking coffee in the viewing room just inside the main entrance, where the chairs were comfortable and the heating effective. Hicks was tired. He had arrived home late the previous evening after seeing the body dispatched to St Paul's and dealing with the paperwork. His clothes were still damp and his wife said his suit was ruined. He'd slept badly, knowing he had an early start at the hospital and thinking constantly of the macerated wrist and the handcuffs and what it would be like to drown in a relentless incoming tide. He woke with a sore throat.

"Morning sir," he said. "We've got an unusual one for you today."

Angus was a tall, heavily built Scot with faded ginger hair, which now, only a few years from retirement, was almost completely grey. His pale blue eyes had seen most of the nastiness one human could inflict on another—but perhaps not everything, he thought as he listened to Hicks' description.

"You mean he was handcuffed to the wreck and left to drown?"

"Looks like it."

"For God's sake! So it's a Home Office job."

Hicks nodded. "I've phoned Cambridge. Dr Foster could be here first thing this afternoon. But we need to get on with identification, so I'd appreciate a look. Nobody local's been reported missing. We emptied his pockets last night and found nothing, but everything was sodden and I suppose we could have missed some papers."

"We can't touch the body till David arrives," Angus said, heading down the corridor to his office to change. "I'll phone him now. But you can search his pockets again."

Angus' office was the first on the right after the viewing room. Tracey had an office beyond this, and the next door led into the post-mortem examination room itself. The corridor continued as a flight of steps with a door at the top. Through this was an open viewing gallery. Hospital doctors came here to check if their diagnoses had been correct or to seek an answer to their puzzling failures. They would see their patient lying naked on one of two stainless steel tables with perforated surfaces so blood and other fluids could drain away into a container when the body was opened. Each table had a built-in sink at the head end and a bright light above. There were two large sinks under the gallery, and on the draining board of one was a set of scales for weighing organs. A further door opposite the entrance gave access to the fridges. Tracey opened this now. Along the wall across from her were eight heavy metal doors, each of which could be opened individually to reveal four body trays in fridges kept between two and four degrees. She opened the door on the left. One of the four occupants was in a green body bag, and she selected this, pulling the tray out head first onto a waiting trolley.

Angus had appointed Tracey ten years before, not without misgivings because of her appearance, but she had been the only candidate, the mortuary attendant's post not attracting many applicants. She was short and squat with close-cropped yellow hair and a ring of barbed wire tattooed around her neck. But she had quickly proved her worth. She was a fast learner, unfazed by the gruesome nature of a post-mortem, by the acrid smell of formalin or the cold, flat smell of death. And she was surprisingly good with the distressed relatives who came to the mortuary to identify or view a body, too dazed perhaps to be alarmed by her appearance.

Hicks helped her move the body onto the autopsy table and she unzipped the bag from the top down. They looked at the man's battered face.

"My God," Tracey said. "Oh Christ!"

She ran off, returning at once with Angus, who came to the table and stared at the body.

Hicks saw the shock on his face. "Is something wrong?" he asked.

"It *is* Jimmy," Angus muttered.

"Jimmy? You know him?"

Tracey answered. "He works here. He's a consultant. Jimmy Greenhalgh."

Angus walked back to his office. He sat behind his desk and struggled to compose himself. After a few minutes, Hicks knocked and came in.

"I'm sorry to press, sir, but you're really sure it's this Jimmy Greenhalgh? I mean, his face…"

"I've known him for fifteen years."

"He was never reported missing, was he?"

"He would have been if he hadn't come back today."

"Come back from where?"

"He didn't turn up for his afternoon clinic the day before yesterday. That wasn't like him. He didn't come home that night and wasn't at the hospital yesterday. Angela phoned me in the afternoon."

"Angela?"

"His wife. My wife and I spent yesterday evening with her and then stayed the night as she was on her own."

"Had he done this before?"

Angus shook his head. "Not that I know of."

"Why did she take so long to report it?"

"I think she didn't want to make a fuss. Perhaps he'd forgotten to mention a meeting at the College in London. Or he'd told her and she'd forgotten. Oh Christ, I don't know. How on earth can I tell her this?"

"No," Hicks said quickly. "Leave that to me. I'll go there now."

He returned in the police car two hours later with a policewoman and a frightened, disbelieving Angela. Angus came with her into the viewing room, holding her hand as she formally identified her husband. Tracey had worked wonders on the empty eye sockets, closing the lids over glass implants, and hiding the macerated wrist beneath the sheets.

Dr David Foster arrived at St Paul's at two o'clock, having driven over from Cambridge, and went straight to the mortuary. He was a short, thin, dapper man with wispy sandy hair and a grey suit with a blue-spotted silk bow tie. Hicks was there already, and Angus was waiting for him. They had talked on the phone and he knew the identity of the body.

"I'm sorry about this, Angus," he said. "You don't need to be present." Normally, in his own mortuary, Angus would have attended a forensic post-mortem. "I'll find you as soon as I'm done."

Foster changed into surgical greens and a full-length plastic apron. He pulled on rubber gloves and white surgical boots and went into the post-mortem room. He looked first at the handcuffs, which Hicks had brought in a clear plastic evidence bag and placed on the stainless steel draining board by one of the large sinks.

Hicks showed him the key. "This opened the handcuffs" he said, and explained where he had found it. Foster broke the seal on the bag.

"I don't know this coast," Foster said. "Can you fill me in?"

"I suppose ideally we should have asked George Peters to be here," Hicks said. "He's the senior coastguard who was first on the scene after the body was discovered. But he's a sarcastic sod and best avoided. Anyhow, I can tell you what you need to know. The beaches are mainly sandy and flat, so the tide goes out a long way and comes in fast. The wreck, or what's left of it, is buried in the sand on Massingham Beach, about four hundred yards from the shore and the sand dunes. The story is that it's been there since the war."

Foster closed the handcuffs, and then opened them easily with the key. He looked carefully with a magnifying glass at the teeth on the ratchet.

"Maybe sand, maybe tissue. Was the key too far away for him to reach?"

"Far too far, if he was handcuffed. And the entrance to the hole it was found in faced obliquely away from him, so he couldn't have thrown it in."

Foster weighed the key in his palm. "It's a solid little thing. How high was the hole above the sand?"

"At least four feet. I can't see that it would have washed in there"

They considered the possibilities.

"I suppose it *could* have been suicide," Foster said. "He might have gone down there, opened the handcuffs with the key, put it in the hole, walked away, snapped the cuff on his wrist and the other half to the strut and waited for the sea. Or it was murder. He was taken there and handcuffed. Maybe the key was put there to taunt him. But he's a big man to drag struggling across four hundred yards of sand in daylight, so he would have had to have walked willingly to the wreck with his killer, who assaulted him there and handcuffed him when he was too dazed to resist. Where would you get handcuffs like these? Are they police issue?"

Hicks shook his head. "Similar but not ours."

"Bondage catalogues have them," Tracey said, blushing deeply when they stared at her.

Foster carefully examined the body. Shoes, socks and trousers were missing, presumably ripped off by the strong tide. The jacket sleeves of the pinstripe suit had ridden up to both elbows over a white shirt. His face was bruised, the nose obviously broken. There was a deep, three-inch slash across his forehead and a contusion on the left temple. Tracey had managed to conceal most of this with makeup, which she now washed off. He lifted the eyelids and removed the implants, revealing empty sockets.

"Crabs, possibly, maybe seagulls when he was exposed on the sand." Foster looked enquiringly at Hicks. "If he went underwater the afternoon he didn't turn up for his clinic, he would have surfaced twelve hours later, early next morning when the tide went out, and that was when the birdwatcher found him?"

Hicks nodded.

"Then he would have gone under again and resurfaced before you found him. Is that right?"

Hicks agreed.

"So we're looking at twenty-four hours at the most underwater, less of course the time when the tide was out and the wreck was exposed. I gather you had to force his arm to his side to get him in the body bag even though it's obviously dislocated, so rigor mortis was present then. It usually subsides forty-eight hours after death, although the cold might slow it down." He attempted unsuccessfully to flex the neck. "Still stiff."

"What about these wounds? Before or after death?"

"Difficult. If there was blood around them we could assume he was still alive when they were inflicted, but of course the sea's washed him clean. Okay, Tracey." He nodded to the mortuary technician, who selected a long pair of scissors from a stainless steel trolley beside the autopsy table and skilfully cut the remaining clothes away.

The suit jacket had ridden up over the body's neck, but when it was removed, they could see brown stains on the shirt collar.

"I'm sure that's blood," Foster said. "And if it is blood, we can assume he was alive when those wounds were inflicted."

"But I suppose he could still have been dead when they handcuffed him to the wreck?"

"Let's hope so. Have you seen a drowning post-mortem before?" Foster asked, and Hicks shook his head unhappily. "When you're drowning in the sea you hold your breath as long as you can and then make a big, involuntary, uncontrollable gasp, sucking salt water into the air spaces in your lungs. Sea water is more concentrated than blood, so fluid is also sucked into the air spaces from the blood passing through your lungs, and they become waterlogged. Without oxygen, you lose consciousness quickly and die in a few minutes. But sometimes, especially if the water is very cold and immersion is sudden, the shock causes the throat to go into spasm, preventing water from reaching the lungs but also preventing oxygen, and reflexly stopping the heart. It's always been hoped that that's how many of the *Titanic* passengers died."

"So somebody who dies from immersion in the sea may have lungs full of fluid or no fluid at all?"

"Exactly. That's why it can be difficult."

When the body was naked, Tracey turned it over, but there was no further information to be gained from examining its back. As she turned it again, she slipped a wooden block beneath the shoulder blades so the chest was lifted from the slab. Hicks had attended post-mortems before and knew what was coming, the sights and the smells. He excused himself. Tracey told him to use her office, and he left with relief.

Foster made the standard Y-shaped incision with a sharp knife, starting at each shoulder, meeting in the middle of the lower chest and continuing down the belly. He peeled the flesh back from the chest, exposing yellow fat beneath. He cut through the ribs with shears and lifted the whole front of the rib cage clear, exposing the heart and lungs and freeing them with a few scalpel cuts. He eased them from the body as one and carried them across to the sink. Normally when the rib cage is removed, the lungs collapse, but these were distended and heavy.

First Foster cut the heart free, weighing it and opening its blood vessels. It was healthy. He turned his attention to the lungs, which were clearly waterlogged. Fluid seeped out as he cut in, and then a tiny piece of green weed appeared, and then another. He opened the stomach. It contained sand and seaweed, which could only have been swallowed when Jimmy was alive.

Foster took the circular saw from Tracey and opened the skull. The brain was undamaged, no contusions or bleeding that might have caused unconsciousness before he drowned.

He removed his gloves and blood-soaked apron and changed out of his greens. Meanwhile, Tracey bundled the organs back into the body cavity and began to stitch up. Angus was waiting for him in his office.

"I'm sorry, Angus, but I'm afraid he definitely died from drowning. There was weed in his airways which he must have inhaled, and sand and weed in his stomach. There was a nasty wound to his forehead, his nose was broken and his skull cracked over the left temporal bone, so he was obviously hit twice with some force and could have been knocked unconscious, but we can't know that for certain and there was no bleeding within his skull or obvious damage to his brain. There was blood on his collar, so the wound had bled, meaning of course that it was caused before death and not by banging against the struts of the wreck after drowning."

Angus shook his head. "I can't believe any of this. What do you think was the sequence?"

"At a push, it could be suicide. He might have put the key in the hole and snapped the handcuffs on himself so he couldn't reach it if his courage failed him. But then he'd hardly hit himself on the head and break his own nose."

"Jimmy wouldn't kill himself; I'm sure of that. I never knew him depressed, and he was his normal self when I last saw him two days ago."

"In which case he was murdered, beaten either at the wreck or before being taken to it. What a vile way to kill somebody."

Angus stood up. "Thanks for coming over, David. It can't have been easy for you either."

They shook hands.

"I'm very sorry, Angus. I know you were old friends."

CHAPTER THREE

Jimmy's father was a GP in Norwich, as was his father before him, and the family never doubted that he would follow in their footsteps. He entered St Stephens Medical School in 1964 when he was eighteen and qualified five years later.

St Stephens considered itself a cut above other medical schools. It was one of the oldest, founded in 1550, and its location across the Thames from the Houses of Parliament reinforced its sense of superiority. It had formally become part of the University of London in 1948 but saw no reason to get involved in university life other than for final examinations. There were sixty students in Jimmy's year, five of them female, a normal proportion at that time. St Stephens' criteria for student selection might seem strange by today's strict academic standards, but at a time when the therapeutic advances of the second half of the twentieth century were just beginning, medicine was still thought of as an art as well as a science and interview committees were as much interested in personality as academic certificates.

He had gone up on the train to London from his boarding school in Somerset wearing a suit and uncomfortable new shoes and anxiously rehearsing the questions he expected to be asked at interview. He waited his turn with five other applicants in a windowless anteroom. He was last to be called and followed the hospital secretary into the boardroom where the other two members of the interview panel sat. The secretary was an elderly man wearing a stiff collar and hospital tie, pinstripe trousers and a black jacket and waistcoat with a gold watch-chain. His white moustache was stained yellow by tobacco smoke. He was trim and upright, not a doctor, an ex-military man. He returned to his place behind the boardroom table between the other two members of the panel. On his right was a fat man in a smart grey suit with Brylcreem-flattened black hair, largely concealed from Jimmy by *The Times* newspaper. He was introduced by the secretary as dean of the medical school. The other panellist, on the secretary's left, was the professor of anatomy. He wore a stained white lab coat emitting a strong whiff of formaldehyde. He was clean-shaven with a ruddy, angry face, bulgy eyes and closely cropped bristly grey hair.

The dean began the questioning. He put down *The Times* and looked at Jimmy. "Are you Jack Greenhalgh's boy?"

"Yes sir, he's my father."

The dean nodded. " I thought you might be. We shared a flat, you know." He was silent for a few moments, deep in thought, drumming pudgy fingers on the table, staring out of the window at the Houses of Parliament across the river. "What's your mother's maiden name?"

"Fiona Carter."

"Excellent. Good show. I always hoped he'd make an honest woman of her." He picked up *The Times*.

It was clear the dean had no more questions, so the secretary turned to the professor of anatomy, who fixed Jimmy with an exophthalmic glare. "Rugger?" he said, in a broad Glaswegian accent.

"I'm sorry?" Jimmy said anxiously.

"Rugger, boy, rugby—you must have heard of it. Like football but the ball's a different shape and you're allowed to pick it up. Do you play for your school?"

"Yes sir, in the first fifteen."

"Position?"

"Wing forward."

The professor leant across in front of the secretary, who flinched at the smell of formaldehyde. "Wing forward, Dean," he repeated.

The dean nodded behind his newspaper. "Good show," he said.

There was a short silence.

The secretary glanced at the dean, who shook his head.

"Well, if there are no more questions, I'll ask you to wait outside for our decision."

"Give my regards to your parents," the dean said from behind his newspaper.

Half an hour later, Jimmy was called in and offered a place.

Next day, back at school, he was summoned to the headmaster's study. Father Pascoe wanted a post-mortem on the interview.

"I've no idea why I was successful," Jimmy said. "I was in and out in five minutes. They only wanted to know about my Dad and rugby. They didn't even ask why I wanted to be a doctor."

"I'm not surprised. You were the last to be interviewed and I'm sure they were bored silly by then. I should think the dean wanted to get back to Harley Street and the professor to his dead bodies. In my experience most boys of your age don't really know why they want to do medicine—they just do. You'd have given them the usual platitudes—wanting to help people, wanting to give something back, whatever that could possibly mean at your age. You wouldn't have got as far as the interview if you hadn't fulfilled their academic requirements, so no point in asking you about that. Your father was an Old Boy of St Stephens so they would automatically have favoured you anyway, but it also meant you had been bought up in a medical family and would understand a doctor's life. No false illusions."

"If I'd been a scrum half rather than a wing forward, would they still have taken me?"

"Oh I'm sure they would. That was just the icing on the cake. You haven't heard of the Hospital Cup?"

Jimmy shook his head.

"There are twelve teaching hospitals in London and they all want to win the cup. It's an annual knock-out competition played with legendary ferocity and brutality. I happen to know that St Stephens are the current holders."

"Let me guess then," Jimmy said. "One of their wing forwards has qualified as a doctor and can't play for them anymore?"

"My guess too," Father Pascoe said.

"So really none of it was down to me?"

"Not entirely. They set great store by the headmaster's reference, which tells them much more about you than they could ever learn at interview. I gave you a good one. I said you weren't the brightest boy in the school by any means but you weren't hopelessly thick like most of them and I had no doubt at all that you would make an excellent doctor. Don't let me down."

"Thank you, sir," Jimmy said.

***

Sometimes St Stephens seemed to Jimmy as much a London club as a medical school. Everybody had to sit their qualifying exams after five years, but for those with independent financial means failure was not a disaster. You would be given another chance the next year, and if necessary the year after that. One student, whose aunt had provided in her will for financial support while he was a medical student, spent a decade at the school and continued to play for the rugby team throughout this time. Eventually the school felt compelled to pass him, but to everybody's relief he never practised medicine, hanging around the students' bar and refereeing matches for many years.

St Stephens House was the social centre for the medical school. Situated just behind the hospital, it had accommodation on the upper two floors for students. The ground floor held a large refectory and kitchens. The floor above was a single long room with a bar at one end and a raised stage at the other for the annual Christmas Review. Leather armchairs and sofas were scattered around, newspapers were free, and the half dozen Bridge tables were usually occupied by students in sports jackets and ties, many of them smoking cigarettes or pipes and nursing a pint of Tartan Bitter.

After eighteen months studying anatomy, physiology and bio-chemistry, Jimmy moved on to the wards and saw patients for the first time. The medical hierarchy was explained to him. At the top of the tree was the consultant. His most senior assistant was his senior registrar, below him was a junior registrar and below him a senior house officer. At the bottom of the pile were one or two housemen, newly qualified doctors in their first year of practice. The consultant's team was referred to as his "firm", and in a teaching hospital half a dozen or more medical students would be attached to each firm for a few months before moving on to a different speciality.

St Stephens had Nightingale wards. These were originally de-signed by Florence herself to allow nurses a clear view of all the patients. There were fifteen beds down opposite sides and a cen-tral area with a large desk and upright, uncomfortable chairs where nurses sat with their paperwork when they weren't busy with pa-tients. Jimmy had noticed Angela around the hospital, pretty in her student nurse's uniform, but had not yet plucked up the courage to speak to her, although he had found out her name and which ward she was working on. The nurses' rota was posted in a utility room off the ward, and he checked when she was next on night duty. Medical students were expected to know everything about patients allocated to them so he had an excuse to visit the ward at any time, although Angela was surprised to see him at midnight. The ward was dark, lit only by the lamp on the nurses' table, where she sat alone. Her supervising staff nurse was taking a short break in the ward kitchen where there was a comfortable armchair. He thought of a line from a song popular in the Christmas show: *"Lady, won't you light your lamp for me?"*

"How's Mr Smith?" he asked.

"He's fine. Going home tomorrow. Why have you come to see him in the middle of the night?"

He took a deep breath. "Actually, it's you I've come to see."

27

"Oh really," Angela said, blushing. She had also noticed him around the hospital. "Would you like a cup of cocoa?"

He had a successful student career. He played in the first fifteen throughout his time at St Stephens and was captain during his last year. The medical school retained the Hospital Cup for two more years, losing it eventually to Barts in a close match in which the independent referee was agreed by all at St Stephens to have been hopelessly biased.

He qualified in June 1969. He and Angela were married a month later at her home in Winchester, and shortly after that he started his first job as houseman to a physician in Southampton. A house surgeon post followed and then two years as a medical senior house officer. He returned to St Stephens in 1972 as a junior medical registrar.

Trainee doctors see their consultant in all his moods. If they admire him, they adopt his way with patients and his approach to diagnosis and treatment. If they don't admire him, they keep it to themselves. Progress up the junior doctor's ladder was entirely dependent on support from their bosses. A bad reference, which might only be the product of a personality clash rather than poor performance, could wreck a career.

When Jimmy was a registrar, his consultant, John Dickerson, was in his early sixties, not far from retirement. All through his long career he had been guided by the axiom "primum non nocere", first do no harm, and he drummed this repeatedly into Jimmy. "The history of medicine is a story of ineffective and often dangerous treatments and operations, and while we laugh at the antics of our predecessors, there is no reason to believe that in years to come our successors won't be laughing at us. We have properly conducted drug trials these days which should allow precise assessment of a new treatment's effectiveness, but when the results are published, side effects are often ignored or glossed over. There is no justification for prescribing a treatment which might be more unpleasant than the illness. Never forget there are worse things in life than death, and always remember as a consultant that the buck stops with you."

Most trainee doctors at some point have a senior they particularly admire. John Dickerson was Jimmy's, and this advice shaped his medical practice.

He progressed steadily up the junior doctor's ladder until eventually, in 1980, sixteen years after entering St Stephens as a student, he became a consultant in Market Houghton, where he would be a physician for fifteen years until his death at the wreck.

PART TWO:

JUNE 1995

SIX MONTHS BEFORE JIMMY'S DEATH

CHAPTER FOUR

Like many Norfolk beaches, Massingham extended inland to a staithe, the old name for a wharf, where quite sizeable ships could load and discharge cargo at high tide. Over the centuries these natural harbours had silted up with sand and mud, but some could still be accessed at high water, playgrounds for dinghies and small yachts. Massingham Staithe was one of these.

Jimmy Greenhalgh kept his yacht *Felicity* there on a mooring. She was big enough to sleep on comfortably but small enough to be handled by one man, and he often sailed alone. The harbour emptied completely as the tide went out, but her twin keels allowed her to sit upright on the sand. It was only possible to sail for a few hours around high water, but a more adventurous alternative was to leave at the height of one tide and return on the next. That way he could sail all day if the tide times were right, but once out at sea had to stay there for several hours until the harbour filled again.

He was planning a sail one summer evening when he met Frances Swynnerton, the senior hospital pharmacist, on her way out of the hospital and she asked politely about his plans for the weekend. "Don't you sail with Angela?"

"She never wants to sail with me." He smiled at the memory of their one and only trip together, when he had misjudged the tide and grounded *Felicity* on the mud. Angela had been in a rush to get back to the children, so he lowered her over the side to walk ashore while he waited for the boat to float off when the tide returned. It had taken her half an hour to plough her way to shore through the mud, and then she had a long and very public walk back to the car. He knew she was secretly pleased to have an acceptable excuse never to sail again.

"I've sailed a bit in the past," Frances said. "I'd be happy to crew for you if you're ever stuck."

Jimmy looked at her in surprise. He hardly knew her. She had only been at St Paul's for a year, and he remembered interviewing her for the post of senior pharmacist. She had come with excellent references from her previous hospital. He remembered that her husband had died unexpectedly, he couldn't recall the details, and she'd wanted a fresh start away from her memories. He thought there were no children. One of her referees had been an old friend of Angus Wilson's, and Angus had invited her to dinner to meet some local people shortly after she arrived. She had become friendly with the Wilsons, and Jimmy and Angela met her there occasionally.

"Come tomorrow if you want," he said, surprising himself, "but it will have to be an early start. Seven at the clubhouse, and we should be back by midday."

"I'll bring a picnic," Frances said.

Driving home, he wondered what had got into him and what Angela would make of it. He was nearly sixty now and Frances was quite a bit younger, mid-thirties he would have guessed. But when he told her, she didn't mind at all. Jimmy had never been unfaithful to her and she had long ago stopped worrying that he might be. She had her own plans for the following day, shopping in Norwich with Mary Wilson, and she was pleased that he had found somebody to take in his bloody boat. She had an abiding anxiety that he would try to interest her in sailing again.

Frances was already there when he parked beside his dinghy next morning. He attached the heavy outboard motor, and she helped trundle the boat to the water's edge. She was tall and slim, only a couple of inches shorter than Jimmy, with a handsome rather than pretty face. Her full lips, rather prominent nose and blue eyes would have been framed by long blonde hair had it not been tied up for the occasion. A navy sweater and tight blue jeans showed off her figure nicely. Jimmy was tall, dark, heavily built but not much overweight, with only a few grey streaks in his thick black hair and a flat tummy which he accurately ascribed to genetics rather than healthy living.

Like most tidal basins Massingham Harbour was protected by a bar of sand. Water trickled past this in gullies and channels when the tide was out and surged over it when it returned. It swirled strongly around Jimmy's boots now as he helped Frances into the dinghy. His boat was moored a few hundred yards down the harbour towards the bar, and the outboard motor struggled against the incoming tide, but in five minutes they were alongside *Felicity*. He helped Frances aboard and they prepared the boat for sailing, stowing their picnic, taking off the sail cover, starting the engine and finally casting off the mooring and motoring towards the open sea. Frances seems clueless and he wondered about her previous experience, but she was eager to help and learnt quickly. The sea was choppy as they crossed the harbour bar, but further out the motion was easier and they hoisted the sails and stopped the engine. This was one of the magic moments of sailing for Jimmy. In the sudden silence he could hear the sound of wind and waves for the first time, and the cries of the terns diving into the sea around them. He inhaled the fresh, salty air. It was turning out to be a beautiful day. An early mist had lifted and the sun was already strong. The deep blue of the sea was flecked with the white of small breaking waves, and the sand dunes on the beach on Tern Island were golden.

Frances went below to make coffee at the small galley and returned wearing tight denim shorts which he tried unsuccessfully to ignore.

"What are those things Jimmy?" She pointed to three black balls on a post of black metal sticking up from the sea a few hundred yards away from them.

"They mark the superstructure of a wreck. When the sea is right out it's completely dry with most of the hull buried under the sand.

It's a menace when you're sailing and it's underwater. The tide seems to drag you towards it. I always imagine there are sirens in it singing especially for me."

Frances shivered. "Let's get away from here."

The wreck was well behind them when the radio crackled into life on Channel 16. This was the emergency channel, constantly monitored by the coastguard and listened to by all sailors.

"Yarmouth Coastguard, this is yacht *Altimeter*, do you read me? Over."

"Yacht calling Yarmouth Coastguard. Go to channel 67. Can you spell your name please, sir."

"Alpha, Lima, Tango, India, no Indium, no Indigo—oh sod it. I-M-E-T-E-R. My engine has broken down. Request assistance."

"It's the Housens," Jimmy said, grinning. "In trouble again."

"Alternator, this is Yarmouth Coastguard. Can I have your position please."

"Not sure exactly but somewhere off Massingham Beach."

"Alternator, are you *Altimeter*?" said the coastguard suspiciously.

"I just told you I'm *Altimeter*! I need a tow. How long will you be?"

Jimmy reached for the microphone. "Yarmouth Coastguard, this is yacht *Felicity*. We are in the vicinity and will look out for *Altimeter*."

"Thank you, sir. The Wells lifeboat is on its way."

"How exciting," said Frances. "Do you think they're in serious trouble?"

"You can never tell with the Housens. They wander the Wash in a battered old houseboat with an unreliable engine and no idea of navigation. Let's see if we can find them."

An hour later they sighted *Altimeter* rolling gently in the calm sea.

"Are you all right?" Jimmy shouted across.

"Hello, Jimmy. We're fine, thank you—just a spot of bother with the engine. We've organised a tow."

Just then the tow arrived in the form of the Wells lifeboat, bristling with seamanship and efficiency. Mr Housen and the coxswain greeted each other like old friends and within a few minutes had secured a line and set off for Wells Harbour.

"We'd better get back quickly too, or Massingham Harbour will be dry," Jimmy told Frances. But the wind was dying and they made slow progress against the tide. An hour later, he knew they had left it too late.

"What do we do now?" Frances asked anxiously.

"We've got seven hours to wait before the harbour starts to fill again. Do you mind?"

"No, I don't." She smiled at him. "Do you?"

"The sea's calm now. We'll anchor off Tern Island and have our picnic."

Jimmy opened white wine and Frances unpacked sandwiches and a quiche. They sat in the cockpit in the strong midday sun, listening to the sounds of the tern colony on the island. There wasn't a soul in sight.

Frances stretched out on the cockpit cushions, drowsy in the heat. "Why don't you stop staring at my legs, Dr Greenhalgh, and do something about it?" she murmured.

A seal popped its head out of the water fifty yards away and stared at them with big, liquid eyes.

He grinned. "I knew you were going to try and seduce me as soon as you got on the boat."

"And I knew you could have used the engine if you'd really wanted to get us back in time!"

CHAPTER FIVE

Felicity returned to Massingham Harbour on the incoming tide. Jimmy had called Angela on his mobile phone in the afternoon to explain that they had missed the tide and wouldn't be back until evening. She wasn't concerned, just relieved that she hadn't had to spend a day at sea herself.

"I've enjoyed it very much," Frances said, smiling. "All of it!"

"Perhaps we'll do it again one day soon?"

"Let's make it very soon."

Felicity adapted well to her new role as floating love nest. The seats in the cabin folded down to make a comfortable double bed; there was a one-ring Calor gas cooker and a small fridge to chill the wine. Jimmy sailed every weekend when tides and weather allowed and occasionally visited the boat in the evening after work. Whenever possible Frances came too, now established in the eyes of his Massingham friends as his regular crew. He was uncomfortably aware that Angela trusted him so completely that he hardly had to make an effort to deceive her, but he submerged his guilt in the fresh excitement of the affair.

He was intrigued by Frances' past, but she told him little about it:

"I was happy, but my life now revolves around you and St Paul's, and I'd rather think about the present."

Jimmy didn't press her, although he learnt a bit. She had worked in a number of hospitals since qualifying as a pharmacist and had only really settled at the last one, where she had stayed for five years. There had been affairs but none of them had lasted. She had always seen herself as a career girl, had never wanted children and, in her late thirties, was happily resigned to living alone. Then, three years ago, she had met her husband, a local solicitor and a bachelor a few years older than herself. They had fallen in love, and to the surprise of both of them were married within a few months. Their increasingly happy life together was shattered by his death in a road accident, and shortly afterwards, almost exactly a year ago, Frances had come to St Paul's.

When the sea drained out of the harbour and *Felicity* was high and dry, her twin keels kept her upright on the sand. One of Jimmy's great pleasures was to spend the night on her and wake to the sound of the incoming flood sloshing and gurgling around the hull. He never lost the excitement he experienced when the boat suddenly floated and spun round on her mooring to face the tide. Occasionally, if Angela was away, Frances would come and they could spend a whole night together. One evening as they lay in bed between lovemaking and sleep, they discussed again an outbreak of meningitis in March, now two months past. Six patients had been admitted to St Paul's under Jimmy's care and they had all died. That day, Frances had received her final confirmation that there had been no problem with the penicillin production process.

"So there was definitely nothing wrong with the penicillin on the ward," Jimmy said thoughtfully.

He remembered the evening he had discovered the damaged ampoules. He had become increasingly concerned with each death, and one evening, when five patients had already died, he had returned late to the ward to visit the sixth, a twenty-five-year-old man with relatively mild meningitis. Treatment had been started in time, and there was no reason why he should not recover completely.

He'd been surprised to find Sister Murphy on the ward, long after her day shift was over.

"I've come in to give the penicillin," she said. He knew she lived close to the hospital in a house she shared with her friend Sister Kenny. "I've been so worried by all the deaths that I've given most of the doses myself."

Jimmy watched her draw four millilitres of sterile water from a glass vial into a syringe and inject it carefully into an ampoule containing white penicillin powder, which she shook vigorously until it had all dissolved. She repeated the process with three other ampoules and then drew the antibiotic solution from all four into a large syringe. They walked together down the quiet, darkened ward to the patient, and she injected it slowly through a rubber bung in the drip tubing straight into a vein. The patient felt nothing.

"I hope it works soon," he said. "My head's killing me."

While Sister Murphy reassured him, Jimmy picked up an ampoule to check the dose. It had a rubber cap secured by a metal rim. The dose, one million units, was correct, but he noticed a tiny vertical scratch on the metal rim. He examined the other three ampoules carefully. All had identical scratches. Two unused ampoules remaining in the box were similarly marked.

He showed the scratches to Sister Murphy, who hadn't noticed them before.

"I can't imagine it's anything significant," he said, "but I'll ask Mrs Swynnerton to look into it tomorrow."

She fetched the notes and he recorded that the patient was stable and described the marks he had found on the ampoule caps. She offered him cocoa before he went home, and they sat in her office discussing problems they had shared in the past. Jimmy had worked at St Paul's for fifteen years but Finoula Murphy had been there for fifteen years before he came. She had been promoted to ward sister five years before he started, and he had thought that by now they had seen it all together. But this meningococcal outbreak, killing every patient, was different.

"Perhaps the bacteria is changing, becoming resistant to penicillin?" Sister Murphy said.

This certainly happened with other bacteria, but not with the meningococcus. Jimmy had seen the cultures in the bacteriology laboratory, and they were all sensitive to penicillin.

"I think we've just been unlucky," he said. "It's a potentially lethal infection and the statistics have caught up with us. I'm sure this chap will survive."

He met Frances in her office first thing next morning and they examined the ampoules together. In better light they could see that the tiny scratches on the metal rim of each lid were identical. She left the office to fetch another box of penicillin from the pharmacy stock, and all the ampoules in it were similarly marked.

"It must be caused by an irregularity in the crimping machine they use to secure the lid," Frances said, "but it's not something I've seen before. I'll get onto the drug company this morning and ask them to check."

"Could you also send these ward ampoules back and ask them to analyse the contents?"

She looked at Jimmy curiously. "Are you worried about the penicillin?"

"I'm not sure."

Now, two months later in the warmth of *Felicity*'s cabin, they relived the next few days. Frances had got in touch with the drug company at once, and later in the day their medical officer had phoned her to confirm that the marks had been caused by their crimping machine and that the fault had already been corrected. The following day he contacted her again with the result of the analysis. All the ampoules contained unadulterated penicillin in the stated dose. Because of Dr Greenhalgh's concern, the company would carry out an exhaustive check on its production line and quality control. When this process was complete, he would send a report of their findings to Frances. This was the information she had just received.

But none of this had helped the twenty-five-year-old man with meningitis on Upper South. It was as though he was receiving no treatment at all. His fever climbed and his headache got increasingly severe until eventually he was crying with pain that even morphine couldn't touch. He slipped into a coma, and forty-eight hours after his admission to St Paul's, three days after he first became ill, he died quietly with his wife and young son by his bedside.

Frances plumped her pillow and sat up in bed. She looked down at Jimmy. "I've been thinking," she said seriously. "We know the penicillin was OK, so there's really only two possibilities: either the patients were just unlucky despite getting the right treatment—or it wasn't being given."

Jimmy stared. "Of course it was being given. You know we checked the drug chart and every dose had been signed for and injected at the right time."

"It sounds daft, I know. There's certainly no doubt that something was injected."

"You mean somebody was deliberately not giving the antibiotic? Giving something else?"

"It wouldn't be the first time."

"It can't be that. Sister Murphy gave most of the injections during the day. She even came in in the evenings to give the last one."

Frances gave him a worried look and said nothing.

Jimmy stared at her. He thought of the devastation of a death from meningitis.

"That's unthinkable!" he said.

***

Finoula Murphy was a sister of the old school, a relic from the days when a career nurse's greatest achievement was to have her own ward. She had been recruited thirty years before by the matron of St Paul's, who had come to her hospital in Westport in the west of Ireland. In those days most district hospitals had their own nursing schools and the students would work on the wards, but it was often difficult to recruit qualified nurses. Irish girls, especially country girls, made good practical nurses. Matron had dressed for the occasion in her dark blue polka dot uniform with a large silver belt buckle and tall starched cap. She came across as imposing but kindly, and Finoula, who had never been outside Connemara in her life, was excited by her description of St Paul's and Market Houghton. She had come with her best friend, Eileen Kenny, and both had remained happily in the hospital ever since.

Ten years after they came to St Paul's, they became sisters with their own wards, Finoula's a medical ward and Eileen's surgical. They never married, and to some extent their personalities developed to mirror the consultants they dealt with. Surgeons were alpha males, often with overbearing self-confidence, and twenty years of dealing with their foibles and tantrums had imbued Eileen with a strength of character that wouldn't tolerate nonsense. She was tall and thin with short grey hair, and one glare from over her gold-rimmed reading glasses could stop even the most arrogant registrar in his tracks.

Finoula, in contrast, was short and broad with a softer, gentler personality. She was a dedicated practical nurse with little time for modern nursing theory, and although she sometimes despaired of the skills of junior nurses and doctors, she was kind to them.

After a few years they had bought a small house in a cul-de-sac behind the hospital. Although they lived together, they retained their independence. Eileen had the small dining room as her sitting room and Finoula the other downstairs room. They were often on different shifts and ate at different times, so the kitchen space was divided equally between them, each with their own cupboards and drawers.

CHAPTER SIX

"The main lesson from our enquiry and our principal recommendation is that the Grantham disaster should serve to heighten awareness in all those caring for patients of the possibility of malevolent intervention as a cause of unexplained clinical events."
—from the Allitt Enquiry (1992)

Jimmy went straight to the library in the Postgraduate Centre when he arrived at St Paul's the next day. He liked working there. It was bright and airy, open plan, with large windows that looked out over a birch wood. He and Anne Marsden, the librarian, had supervised every detail of its design when the Postgraduate Centre was built. She had softened its modern angles with bright curtains and colourful posters. The brass desk lights on the pine tables gleamed as usual, and he suspected Anne polished them herself.

While she searched for the report of the Allitt Enquiry, he stared into the woods, trying to remember the other aliases of Harvey Nicholas. He had first met him at St Stephens Hospital during a stint as a casualty dresser. He was still a medical student and his job was to shadow the casualty officer, helping where he could and getting out of the way when he couldn't. Harvey Nicholas had been rushed in by the ambulance crew, clutching his stomach in severe pain, which was only partially relieved by the large dose of pethidine they had given him. His abdomen was rigid, hard as a board when Jimmy felt it, with three scars from exploratory surgery at different hospitals in the past, although Mr Nicholas was in too much discomfort to give a detailed history. The surgical registrar agreed with their diagnosis of a perforated duodenal ulcer. An X-ray would usually have confirmed the diagnosis by showing free air in the abdominal cavity, but it was normal. Perhaps internal scarring from previous surgery had altered the picture.

"It must be possible to have a normal X-ray," the registrar said, "and anyway, there's no other explanation for the pain and his rigid abdomen."

But there was another explanation, one that he had never contemplated.

Harvey Nicholas was operated on later that night and there was no sign of a duodenal ulcer. In fact, there was nothing wrong at all. They removed his appendix in passing and the registrar was baffled as he sewed up the wound.

"The abdominal muscles only go rigid like that if there's peritonitis because something has burst inside."

The theatre sister thought she recognised Mr Nicholas.

"I never forget a tummy." She moved to the top of the table and stared at his face. "I'm sure he's been up here before."

"He's never been seen at Stephens. There are no hospital notes, and anyhow, he says he's just moved to London."

They discussed Mr Nicholas with the consultant at the start of the ward round next day. He listened carefully to the story, studied the X-ray and turned to the registrar with a grin. "I think you've been had."

Harvey Nicholas, alias Peter Jones, alias Mark Spencer, moved from hospital to hospital feigning the signs and symptoms of peritonitis. Most casualty departments knew of him but he was such a good actor and by now knew so much about surgery that he was often undetected. He wanted to be operated on, or at least to be extensively and painfully investigated. It wasn't pethidine that he was after, although that was certainly a pleasant bonus, and it wasn't the challenge of fooling the doctors, although there was a lot of satisfaction in that. If asked why he did it, he wouldn't have known what to say, and in fact he hadn't given it much thought.

The consultant greeted him like an old friend. "Back again, Harvey?" he said cheerfully. "Or is it Peter or Mark today? Trick us into taking many more bits away and you'll be able to call yourself Dorothy Perkins."

Harvey scowled. "I don't know what you're on about."

"You're rumbled," said the consultant, moving on to the next patient.

Later that day, Harvey vanished, stitches and all. Jimmy had met him once more, years later, at St Paul's, still faithful to the retail trade and now called Joe Sainsbury. His scarred abdomen looked like a map of the London Underground, and he accepted his detection with good grace.

In 1951 Richard Asher, a physician and medical writer, proposed the term "Munchausen Syndrome" for patients like Harvey. The real Baron Hieronymus von Munchausen lived near Hanover in the eighteenth century and would have been deeply hurt to know that his name one day would be associated with the likes of Harvey Nicholas. After a distinguished career in the cavalry, he retired to his estate on the banks of the River Weser, where he developed a reputation as an excellent host and accomplished storyteller. He entertained his guests with tales of his travels and army career, embroidering the facts with flights of fantasy which nobody believed for a minute but which were hugely entertaining. In 1789, a booklet was published entitled *Baron Munchausen's Narrative of his Marvellous Travels and Campaigns in Russia*. It was an immediate success and he celebrated his new celebrity at the age of seventy-four by marrying an eighteen-year-old girl, and dying on his honeymoon from a stroke.

Anne handed Jimmy the report of the Allitt Enquiry and he read it with growing disbelief. In 1991 Beverley Allitt, a nurse working on a paediatric ward, had killed three children and one baby by injecting them with insulin and possibly suffocating them, and attacked nine others, some more than once. She had no obvious motive, offered no explanation and was widely reported in the press as suffering from the syndrome "Munchausen by Proxy". In this condition lies and deceit are also used to obtain repeated hospital admissions and investigations, but whereas Harvey Nicholas wished the pain on himself, Munchausen by Proxy sufferers wish it on their children. These mothers invent stories of illness to get their children into hospital and then use different techniques to mislead doctors and keep the child's investigations going. They prick their own fingers and mix the blood with urine samples to suggest kidney disease. They manufacture fevers by rubbing the thermometer or dipping it in a cup of tea. They rub the child's skin repetitively to cause a rash. They add salt to blood samples to alter biochemistry results. Some of the deceptions are so sophisticated that they suggest medical knowledge, and many of the mothers are trained nurses. Quite a few have Munchausen features themselves, and most of them have a history of repeated minor illnesses, often with long spells off work. They are severely disturbed but they aren't killers, and when their behaviour is exposed they go quietly and rarely reappear elsewhere.

Beverley Allitt was different. She had no children herself. She was a murderer. She had nothing in common with the sad, disturbed mothers with Munchausen by Proxy syndrome. She was a psychopathic, motiveless killer, and it was pointless to label her otherwise.

He wondered how the doctors and nurses must have felt. The report suggested that Allitt might have been stopped sooner if a number of clues had been recognised, but Jimmy doubted that this could have happened. Nurses and doctors help patients, they don't murder them, and it would have been natural initially to assume that the first deaths were a series of unfortunate coincidences, especially as there was no hard evidence to suggest otherwise.

One phrase stuck in his mind and would surface repeatedly in the months to come: the report commented on the reluctance of those involved in the Allitt case to "think the unthinkable".

CHAPTER SEVEN

Jimmy's wife, Angela, had invited Mary and Angus Wilson to supper, and the two couples ate in the kitchen. Although it was August, the Aga was lit, there being no other means of cooking, and the door into the garden was open to cool the room. Jimmy and Angus stood outside, drinking gin and listening to the swifts screeching in their last mad dash around the sky. A bat fluttered close to them in the twilight.

"There's been a lot of change over recent years in our profession," Jimmy said. "I think people want to trust doctors, but politicians and the climate they create try to stop them. They're told we're elitist and arrogant, but if they don't think we're on their side we can't function. It's not fashionable today to believe that somebody could actually want to help you, but if patients don't trust our motives we can't begin to. Mostly I provide reassurance, persuading a patient that he hasn't got cancer, that he's healthy, that he can stop worrying. I can't do that if I'm not trusted."

Angela called from the kitchen that supper was ready.

"What's bothering you?" Angus said.

"I've been reading about the Beverley Allitt case. People like her destroy that trust. The damage she did extends far beyond the children she killed."

"She was a one-off."

"Do you remember that meningitis outbreak in March? All six of them died."

"Of course I remember, but you felt then that nothing more could have been done for them." Angus began to walk into the kitchen and stopped suddenly. He turned and stared. "What are you saying?"

"I don't know if I'm saying anything, but just suppose they weren't getting the antibiotic."

"I thought you'd checked that with Frances. I remember you were worried about marks on the ampoules, which turned out to be nothing, but you said she'd had the contents analysed anyway."

"She did and it was penicillin. But supposing it wasn't really being given."

"How could that have happened on every nursing shift? There can't have been a Beverley Allitt on every shift!"

"Angus, I know that Sister Murphy personally supervised most of the injections on the last patient and he was never sick enough to die."

"Finoula Murphy has always had a crush on you," Angela said as she served the lasagna. "Everybody knows that. She can't take her eyes off you when we have hospital parties here. I'm sure she left those food parcels in the porch when I was away that summer."

Jimmy grinned. "Angela went to her mother's with the children for three weeks. Every night when I got home from the hospital, my supper was waiting for me. All I had to do was to stick it in the Aga to warm it up."

"I don't think that's funny at all," Mary said. "If it was her she must have been very lonely. But she's been a feature of St Paul's for as long as I can remember. Are you seriously saying she's gone mad? Has she ever behaved oddly, in all the time you've known her?"

Jimmy shook his head but Angela interrupted. "There was that business with the potassium. Don't you remember? It was a big worry for you at the time, maybe ten years ago?"

Jimmy nodded. "But nothing came of it. We never proved anything about anybody, assuming there was anything to prove."

The other two stared at him.

"Well come on," Angus said. "What happened?"

Jimmy thought for a moment. "Rosie, a very nice lady with a nasty untreatable neurological disease. She had been my patient for a few years as her illness progressed, and I was fond of her. I was impressed by her courage. She was unmarried with no family locally and she was a close friend of Sister Murphy. She had reached the stage where she was bed bound and could no longer be managed at home. Her breathing and swallowing were impaired and she was almost completely paralysed. She was admitted to Upper South, Sister Murphy's ward, for terminal care, with at the most a few increasingly unpleasant and frightening weeks to live." He thought for a while. "We were all upset by her condition—myself, the junior doctors, the nurses and Sister Murphy of course—but Rosie wouldn't give up and she never complained. And then she died, quite suddenly and quite unexpectedly. Normally we would have seen this as a blessed relief, but it happened at a weekend when a locum junior houseman was covering the wards, and he was unaware of her history. Before the on-call registrar could get to the ward and stop the process, he had put out a cardiac arrest call, and when the registrar arrived she was being subjected to the final indignity of intubation and cardiac massage. He stopped this at once, but not before blood had been taken from a cannula previously inserted into her arm."

"And?" Angus said.

"Well, that's the point of the story. Blood analysis showed a potassium of just under ten, enough to stop anybody's heart, healthy or not, which of course is why potassium is one of the three injections used for legal execution in America. The normal level of potassium in the blood is between 3.6 and 5.2. We asked for a post-mortem. I remember you were away at the time, Angus, so your colleague did it. Kidney failure is the usual reason for a high potassium, but her kidneys looked normal and they had definitely been functioning normally when she was alive. Blood clots in the lungs are a common cause of death in patients like Rosie, but there were none and her heart was healthy—it had just stopped suddenly."

"Did you ever find the reason for the high potassium?" Mary asked.

"It was a mystery. She had had blood tests before, of course, and her level was always in the normal range."

"So no explanation?" Mary said.

"Nothing we could prove."

"Potassium levels in the blood are always high after death," Angus pointed out.

"That's because after death as cells disintegrate they release potassium into the blood and levels can get very high, much higher than ten. But the point about Rosie's death is that the sample was taken within a few minutes of her heart stopping, so it's probably a true representation of serum levels at the time of her death."

"What did you mean when you said you could prove nothing?" Angus asked.

"I think you know what I'm getting at. It has to be a possibility that somebody injected concentrated potassium into the cannula in her arm with the intention of ending her life. Ampoules of potassium are kept on the ward for treating patients whose levels are too low, as this is dangerous in itself, but these are *never* injected into a vein without diluting them first in at least half a litre of fluid and then infusing the solution very slowly."

"Do you mean you think she was deliberately killed?" Mary asked, shocked.

"It's all supposition, of course, and I couldn't see at the time how we could ever prove it." He paused. "If I'm to be honest, I wasn't really sure that I wanted to. I've prescribed morphine to ease intolerable symptoms for patients close to death more times than I can remember—prescribed it in a sufficient dose to relieve their suffering and fear, knowing that such a dose could precipitate the end of their life. I have never thought of this as anything other than good medical practice, and I still don't. There was nothing in Rosie's short future other than choking, panic and fear. She had no family, she was in a side room off the ward, often on her own, with nobody to hold her hand other than her close friend Sister Murphy. If she'd told Sister Murphy she wanted to die now and she helped her, was that so bad? I don't know. Do you? You learn quickly in medicine that there are worse things than death"

They were all silent, the lasagna growing cold on their plates.

"Do you actually know that it was anything to do with Sister Murphy?" Mary said. "Did you investigate?"

"I did, of course, but what was I going to find? And don't forget everybody who worked on Upper South was affected by Rosie's illness. Anybody could have done it—or nobody."

"And now you're worried about Sister Murphy again?" Angus said.

Jimmy sighed. "I don't know what I'm saying, but it's a seed that's been planted in my head and it won't stop growing."

"What seed?" Mary said.

"The possibility that she was somehow involved in four meningitis deaths we had recently."

"In that case you can't possibility ignore it. You'll have to talk to somebody in the nursing hierarchy."

"We go back a long way; she's been my ward sister for fifteen years. I can't accuse her of something like this when I haven't a shred of evidence."

"You don't have to accuse her of anything," Angus said. "Just draw their attention to the possibility and tell them you think it's almost certainly nonsense. They can go back through the off-duty and look at the drug charts and come to their own conclusions. If you were right and did nothing and something else happened, you'd never forgive yourself."

"But I really have nothing to go on. If I pass the buck to the nursing hierarchy, I'll have planted the seed in *their* mind and *they'll* be in the position I'm in now: not really believing it but scared of the possible consequences if they do nothing."

"I still think you have to talk to them, Jimmy."

"But even if there's some sort of investigation and she's found to have done nothing wrong, mud sticks. Her reputation will have been destroyed because of me."

***

Wendy Clarke was Sister Murphy's immediate superior. She was ten years younger but had taken the more profitable course in her career, moving into administration a few years after qualifying. Her job was to bridge the gap between the demands of her harassed, underpaid and usually overworked nurses and those of an unyielding and often uncomprehending management. Although she hadn't worked on the wards for over a decade, it was a tribute to her tact and good sense that she was generally respected. Finoula Murphy, who had little time for nurses who didn't empty bedpans, tolerated her.

"You're quite right of course, Jimmy," she said. "We can't ignore it now it's been raised, but it's the daftest suggestion I've ever heard. She may be cantankerous and opinionated, but Finoula's the best nurse in the hospital."

"There were six cases in that outbreak. The sickest two went to intensive care and didn't survive. That's just about acceptable. The other four, the least ill, went to Upper South and we lost the lot."

"I can see why you're concerned," Wendy said, "but it must be chance. I'll check the rota in case there's a common denominator and look at the drug charts to see who signed for the penicillin and I'll let you know tomorrow. But I wouldn't lose too much sleep tonight!"

His bleep went off the following afternoon.

"Come and see me when you've finished," Wendy said. "We need to talk."

His clinic overran by an hour, but she was still waiting in her office. He was tired, and she sat him in the chintzy armchair where too many nurses to remember had poured out their upsets and anxieties to her.

"I wasn't too worried when I came here," Jimmy said as she handed him a cup of tea, "but I am now I'm in the chair. What have you found?"

"She worked all through the outbreak. She had a week's leave booked from Thursday but cancelled it two days before on Tuesday, the day after the second patient died on Upper South."

"Why would she do that?"

"I don't know. She doesn't have to give a reason—she's the boss. She reorganised the rota so she worked day shifts, Monday to Friday, after that.'

"When did the next case come in?"

"Sunday evening. She wouldn't have heard about it until she came on duty at eight on Monday morning."

"So who gave the penicillin?"

"The first dose was given in casualty and the second dose was given at two in the morning by the staff nurse on duty. After that all the penicillin was given by Finoula. He died on Thursday afternoon."

Jimmy exhaled, a long sigh, and sank back in the armchair. They were silent for several minutes.

"What was the normal time of the last evening dose?"

"Midnight, but the times were changed slightly so it was given at eleven. The first morning dose was normally at six. She came back in for the evening one and started early each morning."

"At six o'clock! Didn't anybody comment?"

"She's often come in early in the past."

"So who changed the time of the midnight dose?"

"The houseman, but it was her suggestion. An hour or two either way made no difference. She said it would help the nurses, and he wouldn't have dared question her."

"But surely an intravenous drug is checked by a second nurse?"

"Of course it is, and both nurses have to initial the drug chart, the one who checks and the one who gives it. But the nurse who checks the dose doesn't always watch it being given unless she's supervising a junior." Jimmy recalled the night he had come onto the ward late and found Sister Murphy preparing the penicillin for the last meningitis patient on her own.

"And the last patient?"

"He was admitted a week later on Tuesday at midday. Finoula was on duty. The first dose of antibiotic was given in casualty and she gave the rest. He died on Thursday evening."

He had liked this patient particularly, a painter and decorator with flecks of white paint on his glasses and an easy smile. Jimmy remembered the seven-year-old son who had interrupted on Wednesday to show him a drawing of his dog and ask when his daddy could come home.

"What do we do now?"

"I'm not sure. There's no proof of anything. It may all just be coincidence."

"Do you think it is?"

"I can't decide, Jimmy, but it has to be nonsense. We nurses pretend we know exactly what we're doing, with our flip charts and flow diagrams and guidelines for 'best practice', but I think at heart most of us feel we are floundering when we make our excursions into modern nursing practice. We need to know there is a solid foundation to return to. Finoula Murphy and her friend Eileen Kenny on the surgical ward provide that. We'd be shattered if she was accused of something like this."

"You'll have to talk to her, unofficially at least. Don't accuse her of anything, just chat about the meningitis cases generally and let her know that you realise she gave most of the antibiotics. Perhaps she'll give something away but at least she'll know you suspect her."

"I don't know if that's enough. How did Beverley Allitt's activities come to light?"

"The police were called in, not particularly because *she* was suspected but because there was enough to suggest that the deaths weren't accidental. She was arrested three weeks later."

"You don't think we should involve the police, do you?"

"Of course not." He thought for a while. "But we've got to remember that the Allitt Enquiry criticised the doctors and managers for not acting sooner."

Wendy took a deep breath. "Would you like another cup of tea?"

Jimmy shook his head, and neither spoke for a while.

"We're going to have to inform the chief executive," she said.

***

St Paul's Hospital had recently become St Paul's Hospital Trust. The government had decided that hospitals were businesses competing in a market for custom like any factory. Factories made cans of baked beans and hospitals made "Consultant Episodes". Managers were drafted in from the world of industry to sort out the National Health Service.

Brian Farrell had been marketing manager for a company making garden furniture. Their fortunes had been badly affected by the slump of the late 1980s and he had applied for a post in the National Health Service at a time when bureaucracy was rapidly expanding. His business experience and grasp of management jargon assured him rapid promotion, and in a very few years he found himself chief executive of St Paul's. Jimmy Greenhalgh thought him intolerable, but acknowledged sadly to himself that, in this new world, Farrell was his boss.

"Come in, Jimmy. Come and sit down. Good to see you."

Farrell had taken the old committee room as his office and slouched behind the long oak desk that had seated Jimmy's interview committee fifteen years before. He noticed that the photos and paintings of retired physicians and surgeons, some long dead, had been removed from the panelled walls and replaced with management awards and slogans.

"We might have a problem. Most likely it's nothing. But I thought you should be aware."

Farrell sat up. "Go on."

Jimmy began to explain but was interrupted straight away. "Not another meningitis epidemic! The local press gave us hell last time. I tried to play the deaths down but they even accused *me* of covering up a major threat to public health. You said the fuss would pass, Jimmy. I hope it's not back."

"It isn't back, I'm talking about the same patients. I don't even know if we have a problem, but I am worried." As simply as he could, Jimmy described the March outbreak with its total mortality. "Most of those patients should have survived."

"But you said at the time that they were just unlucky and we'd done all we could."

"And so we did. And most likely they were just unlucky. But there is another possibility. I don't believe it, and I don't think we could prove or disprove it anyhow, but I want it documented that we discussed it."

Farrell listened carefully while Jimmy explained his anxieties.

"Wasn't there something like this in another hospital?" he asked.

"The Allitt case."

"Christ, I remember that. A mad nurse was killing children and the managers were blamed."

"Not exactly," Jimmy said.

"We've got to suspend her now."

"We can't do that. There's no evidence. It's all supposition."

"Then we've got to suspend her pending an enquiry."

"Don't rush into that," Jimmy said. "Let's discuss it at least."

But it takes two to discuss.

CHAPTER EIGHT

Wendy wasn't surprised by the phone call from Brian Farrell. The Finoula Murphy affair had developed its own momentum; they had pushed the boulder off the hillside and now it was bouncing down the slope. There was a procedure to follow. First she had to talk to Finoula herself, warning her of what was coming. She would then receive a formal letter from the chief executive suspending her on full pay. Farrell would make no specific charges and the letter would be vague. On Wendy's advice, Sister Murphy would contact the local representative of the Royal College of Nursing, effectively the nurse's union, and he would involve the regional representative. Finally there would be a formal enquiry conducted by the chief executive and members of the Trust Board. After that the police might be involved.

Wendy had no idea if all this was sane or insane. She understood Jimmy's anxieties but realised as he did that there could be an innocent explanation for everything. Nobody could dispute that the patients had died from a potentially fatal infection, and so far there was no evidence that Sister Murphy's behaviour was anything other than conscientious. On the other hand, most of the patients should have survived with penicillin, and she had given nearly all the injections herself.

It was mid-afternoon on Upper South, a quiet period with no doctors' rounds and visiting time an hour away. Sister Murphy had just finished showing a student nurse how to clean an incontinent unconscious patient. She noted grimly that the girl had no idea how to move the dead weight of the patient and that every now and again she wrinkled her nose and shuddered at the smell. Her own sleeves were rolled up to the elbows, and wisps of grey hair had escaped from her cap. She was short but strong and wiry, red-faced and slightly breathless with the effort. Her features were coarse, dark and rather masculine, with thick eyebrows and a faint moustache, but her eyes were the pale cornflower blue of Connemara. She had never been pretty but looked competent and kind.

"For God's sake, girl, stop worrying about breaking a nail and pull the end of this sheet. *Pull* it tight, don't pat it!"

Eventually it was done, the oblivious patient parcelled clean and tidy between the sheets, for the moment at least. She sent the student off for a tea break to recover and washed her hands at the sink in the patient's room, thinking about her plans for the evening. It was high tide at seven, a big spring tide, and she and Eileen Kenny were going to take a picnic supper to Massingham Beach and watch it come in. The marshes would flood behind them, and for an hour or two it would seem as though they were on an island.

She had always needed the sea. The flat Norfolk coast with its huge beaches was quite different from the rocky Connemara bays of her childhood, but it was the same sea.

She was surprised when Wendy Clarke came to the ward and asked her to come to her office. There was still a lot to be done before visiting hours, but Wendy was insistent. They took the lift down together in silence. She never bothered with small talk and sat quietly on the upright chair across the desk from Wendy, who had thought hard what to say but still had no idea how to begin.

"Something unfortunate has come up that you're going to have to be aware of. There's been a lot of anxiety about the meningitis deaths on your ward in the spring."

Sister Murphy waited, watching Wendy carefully.

"Nobody can understand why they all died."

She stirred. "No more can I," she said.

"How do you mean?"

"I've had meningitis patients on the ward before, sometimes more than one at a time. I've known a few die but nothing like this."

"Did you wonder about it?" Wendy asked.

"I worried about it, of course, and I tried to give most of the penicillin myself."

"Why did you do that?"

Sister Murphy stared down at her folded hands in thought and was silent for so long that Wendy was about to repeat the question.

"Perhaps it wasn't necessary, but the girls these days make me nervous at times. Their training has changed for the worse, far too much theory and nowhere near enough practical."

"But only qualified staff can give intravenous injections, and they have to get the hospital certificate first."

Sister Murphy glared at her angrily. "You knew I'd given all the penicillin before you got me down here. Is that what this is all about? I'm sure you think it's a bit odd but at least I know they got the antibiotic on time. Anyhow, Dr Greenhalgh knew about it. He came on the ward one evening when I was injecting the last patient, that nice painter, and we had cocoa together and talked about it all." Her face softened at the memory.

Wendy took a deep breath. "It's actually Dr Greenhalgh who raised this," she said, guiltily shifting the responsibility onto Jimmy.

"Dr Greenhalgh." Sister Murphy stared at her in disbelief.

She ploughed on. "He believes that if the patients had really got penicillin they wouldn't have died."

"But he knows they got penicillin. He told me he'd had the ampoules checked by the pharmacy. If you don't believe the doses were correct you can check on the drug sheets."

"We have checked.'

"And?"

"Of course they were correct."

Sister Murphy was beginning to get angry. "I don't understand what you're talking about. Will you please explain properly what this is all about!"

"I haven't been able to find anybody who watched you give any of the penicillin injections to the last three patients."

"I've just told you Dr Greenhalgh saw me!" She was shouting now.

"Please keep calm, Finoula. That was only once."

"Don't call me Finoula," she hissed, leaning forward. "Are you suggesting I didn't give the injections I signed for?"

"We have to check everything," Wendy said lamely.

"Does Dr Greenhalgh believe that?"

"I don't think he believes it, but he was the one who bought it up."

***

After the meeting Finoula had gone straight to her friend Eileen Kenny's ward. It was the end of the shift and they walked home together. She could hardly speak without sobbing, and Eileen, thoroughly alarmed, had to wait until they reached the small semi-detached house they shared on an estate near the hospital before she had any idea what had happened. She settled Finoula in her chair in her sitting room and made tea. By now she had regained some control.

"Eileen, they're going to suspend me!"

"Suspend you?" Her friend stared in disbelief. "What are you talking about?"

Sobbing again, Finoula described her meeting with Wendy Clarke. "They think I only pretended to give the penicillin injections to those meningitis patients who died."

"Only pretended!"

"I didn't trust the nurses to give the injections properly. You know how useless most of them are. I reorganised the times slightly so I could give them all myself if I went in last thing at night and first thing in the morning."

"And they all died!" Eileen was beginning to understand. "You never told me you were giving all the injections yourself. What a daft thing to do."

"Oh Eileen, I suppose it was, but I only did it for the best."

***

It was a dismal picnic. Finoula hadn't wanted to go but Eileen insisted. They would both go mad if they sat in the house that evening, she said. She drove to Massingham Beach in the small Ford car they had bought together. They walked several hundred yards to a spot sheltered from the breeze by low dunes and spread a tartan rug above the flotsam of the last tide.

"It shouldn't reach us here," Eileen said. She opened the picnic basket which contained the usual thermos of tea and pulled out an unopened bottle of Irish whiskey, duty free from the last visit home.

Finoula sipped her plastic cup of Paddy's, watching the relentless creep of the sea towards them across the sand. "I can't go into work again. Mrs Clarke says I'll get a letter tomorrow from the chief executive suspending me. There's going to be an enquiry to see if I can go back."

Eileen stirred the fine white sand with a stick. "All you have to do is show that you gave the injections you signed for. Somebody must have seen you."

"I suppose they'll ask the nurses and then they'll all know," Finoula said listlessly. "They wouldn't watch me because I'm the sister. They won't find anybody who can definitely remember."

Although Eileen could believe this, she couldn't understand how the whole affair had escalated so quickly. "But if nobody can prove you did give them, nobody can prove you didn't!"

Finoula stood up with the help of Eileen's stick and walked unsteadily towards the sea. The white sand gave way to a firm, yellow, ridged beach and then to a patch of soggy mud. She slipped suddenly and sat down. A group of children watched, laughing, as she tried unsuccessfully to stand, sliding and falling again. Eileen ran and pulled her up. Her white skirt was caked, and they tried to scrape the mud off as they walked back to the sand dunes, but it was badly marked.

"Oh leave it," Finoula said irritably. "The skirt's ruined."

"Mud sticks," Eileen thought sadly.

The tide crept in and surrounded them. She put the Paddy's away and they ate their picnic miserably.

"How could Dr Greenhalgh ever believe I would do something like that? How could he? After all those years."

It was a dramatic sunset, but the two women on their sand dune island were oblivious to it. A mile away, the superstructure of the wreck vanished quietly beneath the surface of the calm sea.

***

Dear Sister Murphy,

I'm writing to confirm your suspension from duty on full pay pending an enquiry by the hospital board into the meningitis deaths on Upper South ward. You will be informed of the date of the enquiry in due course. You may be represented at these proceedings by your union if you wish.

Brian Farrell
Chief Executive

CHAPTER NINE

Stansted Airport was less than two hours' drive from Market Houghton. Eileen drove and Finoula felt the usual stir of excitement when they turned off the motorway and she could see the control tower in the distance. Stansted was the gateway to home.

Wendy had phoned a week after the chief executive's letter. The enquiry would take place at the end of September, six weeks hence. In the meantime, Finoula's time was her own but she must contact nobody in the hospital and would be wise to get in touch with her union soon.

"She must be joking," Finoula said. The local representative of the nurse's union was the male charge nurse on Jimmy's other medical ward. "I don't want College Colin knowing my business."

"You're going to have to tell him sometime," Eileen said.

The airport was only recently built, and Finoula loved the spacious open design, the light, airy cleanness of it. Eileen kissed her goodbye and she went through to the departure lounge. The whole of one side of the terminus was glass, and little trams moved silently outside, carrying passengers to and from the planes. The Irish seemed to travel in families, and small groups of several generations were scattered about. Two nuns in black gowns with cream hoods and bibs talked quietly together, and two priests, Guinness in hand, sat silently at the bar.

As usual, Shannonair's flight to Knock International Airport was full. Some of the passengers were pilgrims, but most were just grateful for the cheap, reliable service that took them deep into the west of Ireland. A bog in the middle of nowhere was an unlikely site for a jumbo jet sized runway, but then again the little village of Knock had been a surprising choice for a visit from the Virgin Mary. Finoula bought a litre of Paddy's in the duty-free shop for her brother Dermot and two hundred cigarettes for Sean. The flight boarded on time and soon she was settled in a window seat with the two billowing nuns beside her. All three made the sign of the cross as the plane accelerated, and Finoula only opened her eyes when eventually they levelled out.

"Thanks be to God," the furthest nun muttered.

"Amen," said her friend, winking at Finoula.

The flight was over in an hour. Pretty Irish stewardesses caked in makeup tried half-heartedly to sell duty-free drink and cigarettes to her companions. Suddenly, they were descending towards Knock. Out of the window, she could see the small lakes and scattered bog of County Mayo. They dropped through patchy cloud, buffeted intermittently by the strong westerly wind. The nuns made the sign of the cross again, and she closed her eyes and did the same, and the pilot, fortified by this display of confidence, made a perfect landing.

"Welcome to Knock International Airport".

The sign was hardly visible through the driving rain. Finoula collected her luggage and walked through to the hall of the small airport, where Dermot was waiting.

"Grand day," he said without irony. "Welcome back."

***

It is claimed that on 21st August 1879 the Virgin Mary visited the village of Knock accompanied by St Joseph and St John the Evangelist. She stood motionless against the south gable of the little village church while angels hovered around a lamb standing on a plain altar beside her. Behind them was a large cross. The apparition, which lasted two hours, was lit by a "heavenly" light.

Fifteen people of all ages saw the Virgin, watching in awe until she faded away.

A Church Commission of Enquiry later that year found the testimony of the witnesses "trustworthy and satisfactory", and pilgrims began to stream to Knock. Remarkable cures were claimed and the gable wall of the church was soon covered with crutches and sticks.

Almost one hundred years later, the Horan International Airport was built a few miles from the village, named after the entrepreneurial local priest who was its driving force. Now Catholics travel to the shrine from around the world and the airport has opened up the west of the country to tourism.

Dermot parked against the pavement outside the church, and Finoula hunted in her hand luggage for the empty lemonade bottle, a ritual prop of all her visits home. Before choosing a holy water tap, she walked with her brother to the glass oratory which now enclosed the south gable wall. Dermot was his usual cynical self but she knew he would kneel and pray in total concentration.

"Why ever would she come here with them two and a sheep," he muttered. "Were they looking for Lourdes and got lost in the mist?"

They heard the familiar hum of prayer from the groups of pilgrims who circled the church in all weathers reciting the rosary: *"Holy Mary, mother of God, pray for us sinners now and at the hour of our death."*

The original south wall of the church had been badly damaged by souvenir hunters breaking off bits of plaster. Now it was faced in limestone brick, and in front of this the apparition had been recreated in white marble. The statues were beautiful, pure white broken only by the gold crown on Mary's head. Finoula and Dermot knelt side by side, heads bowed. She told Our Lady about her problems at St Paul's, praying that they would be quickly resolved, preferably without the help of College Colin, and waited for Dermot to finish. He looked incongruous in the chapel in his Garda uniform which he had not had time to change, although he had locked his revolver and handcuffs in the boot of the car.

Holy water was dispensed by a series of taps set in marble carvings of biblical scenes along the wall by the road. Finoula liked the picture of St John the Baptist and Jesus best and always used this tap to get her mother's supply. Dermot held the lemonade bottle for her.

"You might as well fill it from the sink in the ladies," he said, but he crossed himself when some of the water splashed onto his hand.

Their mother still lived in the family cottage close to the village of Keenan at the tip of Killary Harbour, a ninety-minute drive from Knock. Dermot drove well, and Finoula relaxed and enjoyed the familiar scenery. The wind and rain had passed over and the sun shone, drying the deep puddles on the rough Irish road. They drove through Castlebar and on to Westport where they had both gone to school, passing the weathered statue of St Patrick on its tall column in the centre of the town. The nuns had made them learn the inscription at its base and she could still remember it: "I am Patrick," she chanted, and Dermot joined in, "a sinner most unlearned and least of all the faithful and utterly despised by many."

The road sloped down towards the sea and he turned left towards Keenan, twenty miles away.

Northern Connemara is a land of mountains and bog on the edge of the Atlantic. Dark lakes lie in the shadow of brown mountains etched near their summits with vertical silver streams. The bog in the valleys is scarred with peat workings where turf is piled high in tidy black stacks by the roadside. White cottages with a few bent trees around them are scattered haphazardly about. It is not an easy place to live, but those ensnared by its spell can rarely leave it for long.

Connemara is about the weather. It takes first whatever the Atlantic throws at Ireland, usually wind and rain, and diverts and dilutes it before passing it on. Here things happen quickly. A squall will rush in from the sea, drenching the twelve Bens of Clifton and hiding them completely in mist. Half an hour later, the mountains appear again, bright in sunlight and shadowed with infinite variation by the clouds. The view here is never the same, one minute depressing, the next achingly beautiful.

Old Mrs Murphy had lived in the same cottage on the edge of Killary Harbour for fifty years. Her husband's life had started and ended within its four white walls. Dermot and Finoula had walked a mile down the stony track each day to the crossroads at Keenan to catch the school bus to Westport. Their brother Michael had lived all but four years of his life on the bed in the small back room, looking through a red-framed window at the thorn tree on the stony slope.

Dermot drove slowly but the police car banged hard on the rocky ridges of the track.

"Never mind," Finoula said. "You can tell them you were chasing the IRA."

He didn't smile. "She'll be glad to see you. Mother's not frail yet but she's getting old. She does everything for Michael now and she worries what will happen to him when she's gone."

"Of course she does." She looked out from the car across the harbour. Killary was Ireland's only fiord, seven miles long, and the Mweelrea mountain, the tallest in Connemara, plunged steeply down on its north side. She could see two cottages half a mile away across the water and the square frames of salmon farms in the middle. On a tiny sandy beach a hundred feet below, a greater black-backed gull was pecking the eyes from a dead seal.

"It's a long way from Market Houghton," she said quietly.

Old Mrs Murphy was waiting at the door of the cottage. "I could hear you banging down the track a mile away." She hugged Finoula while Dermot looked anxiously under the car for damage. "Quiet now. Michael's asleep."

They tiptoed across the flagged floor of the tiny main room, bending low at the bedroom door. Michael slept peacefully, dreaming of his father's arms about him. Outside the window, the thorn tree tossed in the rising wind.

"It'll be a wild night, I'm thinking."

Dermot, reassured about the police car's bottom, was trying to turn it around, manoeuvring between a steep drop on one side and rocks on the other.

"Careful, Dermot," his mother said helpfully.

He leant out of the window. "Were you planning on seeing Sean?" he asked Finoula.

"Perhaps."

"Don't bother, Finoula. Stay here with your mother and Michael. Don't waste your time."

"Don't forget your Paddy's," she said, handing him the duty-free.

He saw the cigarettes in the plastic bag. "Who are they for?"

"Mind your own business!"

***

Michael woke an hour later. They were sitting at the table finishing their tea when his high-pitched cry began. Mrs Murphy walked quickly to the back room and Finoula followed. He lay on his left side, curled in a ball, head arched back, staring at the window.

"Is it the wind that upsets him?"

"He's used to that." Mrs Murphy slid her arms under his body, turning him towards the room. "He wants company."

Michael's cry changed when he saw Finoula. It became deeper, more gurgly, and he drummed his feet against the bed-board.

"Oh love," she said, gathering him in her arms like a child and hugging him, and he settled at once.

He had wet the bed, and they changed it together. Finoula noted that his skin was intact, no trace of a bedsore. Her mother's nursing had been faultless over the years. They fed him soup and mashed potato and settled him back down again. His mother stroked his hair, humming softly to him until he fell asleep. "He only knows this house, but I won't be here for ever."

Later that evening after her mother had gone to bed Finoula opened the front door and stood outside, breathing the soft, moist

Atlantic air. The wind was strong now and she swayed in the gusts. *There are worse places than this,* she thought.

***

Dermot was eight, Finoula six and Michael four when meningitis hit Keenan. It was the middle of winter and the weather was atrocious. The Westport road had been flooded for several days and Doctor Cunningham couldn't get through, although he gave advice on the only phone in the village. Not that there was much advice to give; he expected meningitis to be fatal without antibiotics. Penicillin had been discovered several years previously but it was still difficult to obtain and he had used up his limited supplies on Westport cases.

Michael went down first. He had been a lovely child, Finoula remembered: red haired, blue eyed, bright and fascinated by everything, and so affectionate. Their father adored him and wouldn't leave his son when he became ill, cradling and kissing him until the fever abated. Michael survived but his brain was badly damaged.

A week later, the meningococcus killed Finoula's father. She sat with Dermot, unnoticed by the turf fire, for two days, listening to his delirious shouting and their mother's murmured reassurances before there was peace in the cottage again.

But that wasn't the end of it. Soon afterwards their Auntie Dolores died in the nearby village of Tully Cross. She had lost her husband two years before in a fishing accident and had struggled alone to rear Sean, their only child. After her death, Mrs Murphy took in the seven-year-old boy.

The meningococcus moved on, leaving the young mother to rear four children, one totally dependent. There was a fishing hotel in Keenan, and she took a day job in the kitchen. Finoula looked after Michael. Dermot and Sean, eight and seven years old, looked after the sheep scattered on the sides of the barren Mweelrea mountain. In the evening when Michael was settled, the weary family worked on their school books. By the time Dermot was twelve, their mother had saved enough to send him on the bus to the nuns in Westport. Sean and Finoula followed later. An American relative, made aware of their plight, sent her a small allowance so she could stop work altogether and devote herself to Michael.

The three children did well. Dermot had always wanted to be a policeman and got the necessary grades without trouble. Finoula had nursed Michael for so long that she thought of no other career, but too many Irish girls wanted to be nurses and when the matron of St Paul's visited Westport on her recruiting drive she signed up without hesitation.

"It's just for the training," she said to her mother. "I'll be back after that."

The Murphy children were essentially practical, but Sean was a different child. There was no room for his romanticism on the Mweelrea hillside but it blossomed in Westport. He became fascinated with the wild myths of Irish history and stayed behind after school in the pubs and clubs of the town, listening to the stories and music and often missing the last bus home.

The two boys grew apart, Dermot increasingly conventional and Sean much more of a dreamer. He was a short, dark boy, almost puny beside Dermot, but Finoula was touched by the intensity of his growing republicanism and the undoubted sincerity in his brown eyes. She recognised a siren call that it would be easy to succumb to but more sensible to resist. They became very close and, if they had not been cousins, might have become closer still.

Sean's school grades were good, but he moved to Dublin to work in a pub and they saw him infrequently after that. He still wrote regularly to Mrs Murphy, always enclosing money but avoiding any details of his life. He kept in close touch with Finoula, however, sometimes staying with her and Eileen on visits to England. If Finoula wondered about his business, she never confronted him.

She had been home for two weeks when she decided to go and see him. Eight years ago he had moved back to Connemara, not to the mainland but to Inishbaron, an island twenty miles offshore. On a clear day she could see his island from the cottage.

The ferry service from Keenan had been in the Flaherty family for two decades. Finoula walked to the village, glad of the exercise. "Will you be going tomorrow, Mr Flaherty?"

He looked at her seriously, a tall, shambling man with a weathered face in a battered three-piece suit and stained, collarless white shirt. "Ah well now, Finoula, we might, but then again we might not."

The ferry usually left at ten, tide permitting, and there was no phone in the cottage.

"I wonder could you be more definite, Mr Flaherty?" she said patiently. "The weather seems settled now."

"It does right enough," he agreed.

"So you'll almost certainly be going?"

Mr Flaherty shifted uncomfortably under this unaccustomed pressure. "I'd say there was every chance we'd be going tomorrow, but then again…"

"You might not." Finoula realised she'd been too long out of Connemara. "I'll come anyway."

"Do that." Mr Flaherty beamed.

Next morning, she kissed her mother and Michael goodbye.

"It's only for the day," she told him. "I'll be back on the boat this evening."

The downhill walk to the village was pleasant in the warm sunshine. The quay dried at low tide, but it was high water now and she could see in the distance that the ferry had been moved from its deep-water mooring and tied up alongside. As she came down the hill, she inhaled the wet smell of fish and rotting seaweed mingled with the scent of peat fires.

"You'll be visiting Sean?" Mr Flaherty said when she bought her ticket.

"Just for the day."

She had the ferry to herself, sharing it with a dozen barrels of Guinness, a tombstone and a small bag of mail. The *Queen of the Isles* was an old motorboat, bought by the Flahertys twenty years ago from an American who had run it aground at the head of Killary Harbour, giving no explanation for his arrival. The steel hull was sound but the engine was terminal. They had repaired it themselves, unable to afford a replacement, and it had run intermittently ever since with no loss of life or property thus far. It thumped reluctantly into action after prolonged cursing from Mr Flaherty's son Kevin in the small engine room. His father took the wheel and they were off to Inishbaron, twenty miles and two hours away.

Finoula joined Mr Flaherty on the bridge, and they waved to Mrs Murphy outside the small cottage on the mountain.

"How's Michael these days?" Mr Flaherty asked.

"Much the same."

They motored down Killary towards the sea, skirting salmon farms and small fishing boats. The water was calm but half an hour later they were out in the open ocean, where the *Queen of the Isles* treated the big Atlantic swells with regal distain, ignoring them as they swept towards her and rising easily above them as they passed. Kevin came up on the bridge, apparently confident about the engine.

"That's a great northern diver!" He pointed to a bird on the water a hundred yards away. "They get driven in towards land by wild Atlantic weather."

Finoula looked anxiously at his father.

"We're safe enough," he told her. "The low isn't due through until tomorrow morning, and we'll be home today by early evening."

It was an exhilarating fairground ride under a blue sky, Guinness barrels flashing in the strong sun. She tried to read the inscription on the tombstone.

"Who's it for?"

"Old Mrs Fogarty. Never left the island all her life. They'll have to dynamite a hole for her."

Two white painted rocks made a transit for the tricky entrance to the harbour.

"Baron's a great place for Sean," Mr Flaherty said, watching Finoula closely. "This is the only landing on the island. The rest is cliffs."

She didn't reply. Kevin left the bridge for the engine room. Entering Inishbaron Harbour was clearly taken seriously. They lined up the two white rocks, heading directly towards vertical cliffs. The captain hummed and muttered to himself, sucking on an empty pipe, and the Guinness barrels, loosely tied on deck, shifted uneasily, but the *Queen of the Isles* held her course. As they got closer, Finoula could see a gap. A huge wave picked them up, rushed them towards it and, with a little help from rudder and engine, carried them through into a perfect natural harbour. Suddenly all was calm.

"There now," Mr Flaherty said happily, swinging sharply to the right to avoid Priest's Rock.

Sean was waiting on the stone jetty to take their lines. She scrambled ashore and they hugged each other.

"I've got lunch waiting for you in the cottage. What time, Ned?"

"No later than four if we're to catch the tide and miss tomorrow's gale."

"She'll be here."

"Don't go without me, Mr Flaherty!"

They linked arms and walked up the slope.

***

Inishbaron island is two miles long and a mile wide. Sean's cottage had been built two centuries ago at its highest point, fully exposed to the Atlantic only sixty metres below. From here he had an uninterrupted view of the whole island and the sea. Six other cottages were inhabited and there were several ruins, grey shells of past houses skilfully built without mortar from local stone. From their vantage point they could see Mr Flaherty and Kevin unloading the barrels of Guinness.

"There's a long winter ahead of us," Sean said.

Finoula laughed. "It's only September!"

Lunch was soup and cheese and they ate it in the front room, looking out over the harbour to the mainland beyond and the holy mountain of Croagh Patrick far away to the left. They talked about Mrs Murphy and Michael and their childhood in the shadow of Mweelrea.

"Why are you back now?" Sean asked when it was almost time to go. "You were only here in July with Eileen. Did you just come to bring me cigarettes?"

"I needed a break."

"So soon? And you've come for a month! How did you get the time?"

She didn't answer. Sean watched her.

"Something's wrong, Finoula. What is it?" he said gently.

The worry in his voice broke down the flimsy barrier of control she had sheltered behind since leaving St Paul's and she began to sob violently.

"My God," he said, shocked, hugging her until she was calmer. "What is it, love?"

"It's nothing, Sean." She shook his arms free. "I'll have to go soon."

"How can it be nothing and have you in this state? You *must* tell me."

"I can't," she said, gazing down at the harbour. "I'm too ashamed."

"Ashamed!"

"It's nearly time."

Below them, the Flahertys were boarding the *Queen of the Isles*.

Sean sighed. "Wait here, then, and I'll see if Ned's ready."

She watched him walk down the slope to the jetty, wishing she had the time and the courage to unburden herself. Sean talked to Mr Flaherty for several minutes, turning often to stare back at the cottage. Eventually she got tired of waiting and went down herself.

"There's a problem with the engine," Sean said.

She could hear swearing from the engine room as the diesel turned over but refused to start.

"But I must get back this evening, they're expecting me."

"We can phone the village and get a message through if we have to. Anyhow, it may start yet."

But the batteries were getting flatter and eventually the engine wouldn't turn over at all.

***

Summer is usually quiet in the West Atlantic but occasionally low pressure systems develop unexpectedly and bear down on the Irish coast. The faster they come the stronger the wind, and this one was moving very quickly. Finoula had been aware of a rising breeze even before they had given up on the ferry, and by evening it was howling dramatically outside the thick walls of the cottage, rattling the windows.

Sean waited until after supper. They were sitting on either side of the turf fire, which smoked intermittently in the stronger gusts.

"It doesn't smoke like that until it's really windy," he said. "It's a gale at least. You'll be here for a day or two before it's safe to leave the harbour."

She smiled, relaxing with her whiskey. "I don't mind now."

"So you've got plenty of time to tell me what it's all about."

She stared into the fire. "I'll tell no one else, Sean, and you mustn't either. They've got problems enough."

He agreed.

"I've been suspended."

He watched her carefully, uncertain.

"There's going to be an enquiry."

"An enquiry into you?" Sean threw another turf on the fire.

"They're suggesting I deliberately killed four patients."

"What?"

"They think I didn't give penicillin to meningitis patients."

"Who's they?"

"Dr Greenhalgh for one."

"But you've worked with Greenhalgh for fifteen years! How could he believe that?"

"I suppose he has to think of everything," she said sadly.

Jimmy's betrayal was the worst aspect of the whole affair for her, but she still wanted to defend him.

"What a bastard," Sean said angrily, banging his fist on the arm of his chair. "We'll deal with him. You leave him to us."

"Be sensible, Sean. He's only doing his job."

"It's not his job to destroy you. Can't you see, he's protecting his back. He knows he's threatened and he's sacrificing you."

"How is he threatened, Sean? You don't know what you're talking about."

"His patients died, not yours. His name was at the top of the bed. He's responsible, not you."

She was silent.

"There's a cover-up, Finoula. Surely you can see that. There's been a cock up with the drugs. They need a scapegoat and they've chosen you. Look, love, you've got to fight this. All you have to do at the enquiry is tell the truth and they'll be forced to look elsewhere. And *then* we'll decide what to do about Dr bloody Greenhalgh."

The storm blew for two days. In that time the island seemed to Finoula to be the best place in the whole world. Huge grey Atlantic waves, bigger than Market Houghton houses, rolled in and smashed on its western cliffs. Sean's cottage was drenched in the spray which blew across the island and soaked the Flaherty's boat in the relative calm of the harbour below. On the second evening, linking arms and leaning backwards against the wind, they walked down to the bar in the cottage opposite Priest's Rock. Ned Flaherty and his son were there, well settled.

"Whatever you want to drink." Ned grinned. "As long as it's not Guinness."

She thought of the barrels on the deck of the Queen of the Isles and said nothing. She drank Paddy's and listened to the songs, hearing how Kevin Barry gave his young life in Mountjoy Gaol for the cause of liberty and how Father Murphy from old Kilcormac leapt up the rocks with a warring cry and how they were hanging men in Ireland for the wearing of the green. Sean led the singing, his face flushed with the unconditional enthusiasm she recognised from long ago.

Afterwards, walking back arm in arm in the fading wind, they sat on a bank of grass and looked out across the water. Sean pointed to a large rock near the harbour entrance. "That's called Priest's Rock. In 1649 Oliver Cromwell led an English invasion of Catholic Ireland. It's said that he tied a Roman Catholic cleric to the rock at low tide and watched him drown. There's a sandy bottom around it and a convenient spike to hitch a rope to."

"What a horrible death!"

Sean agreed. "You'd have to be a right bastard to deserve that."

Next day she awoke to silence. The wind had died. She could see the Flahertys on the *Queen of the Isles* in the harbour below, and shortly afterwards the ancient diesel engine thumped into life.

CHAPTER TEN

Sister Murphy stayed in Ireland for a further week before returning reluctantly to Market Houghton. Even more reluctantly she contacted Colin Smythe, alias College Colin. He was the charge nurse on Upper West, Jimmy Greenhalgh's other ward, and she phoned him there. He agreed without enthusiasm to come to her home after work.

The Royal College of Nursing is the body responsible for standards and education in the profession. It is also the Union to which the majority of nurses belong. Each hospital has an unpaid official, the first port of call for a nurse seeking union advice or representation. As such an official, Colin Smythe had listened to many grievances and complaints, but he was completely unprepared for Finoula's story.

"Good God Almighty!" He stared at her. "I knew nothing of this. They think that you deliberately withheld the penicillin?

"I don't know if they really believe it," she said miserably, "or if they're just covering themselves, but it's nonsense of course and the union's got to sort them out. The hearings in two weeks."

"Two weeks! Why didn't you tell me sooner?"

"I was in Ireland," she said, glaring at him.

Finoula Murphy and Colin Smythe represented two extremes of nursing practice and neither had time or respect for the other's views. She was unashamedly old fashioned while he said she was hopelessly out of date. Colin slavishly followed every modern shift in nursing theory while Finoula muttered to Eileen that he was a trendy idiot. She believed that patients were admitted to hospital to be treated by doctors and cared for by nurses. He maintained that patients were clients, equal partners in the healing process, and insisted they sign a contract of "holistic care" when they were admitted. On Colin's ward, Dr Greenhalgh was an equal member of the 'caring team'; on Finoula's, he was the boss.

This was not a promising basis for the support that she was going to need at the enquiry, and she was relieved when Colin explained that in a matter of this importance he would have to enlist the help of Tony Parsons, the College's regional representative. Parsons was a full-time regional official. She had heard him talk once on medico-legal problems and had been impressed by his common sense. She knew he had been a charge nurse on a medical ward himself in the past. He was of her generation and she thought they would probably think alike. She was further reassured when she met him later in the week. He was grey haired, overweight but distinguished in a dark suit. He looked at her sympathetically, forehead wrinkled over the gold half-moon glasses on the end of his nose. She thought he looked more like a doctor than many of the younger consultants.

"This is completely unacceptable," he said. "I've talked to Wendy Clarke and she says they haven't turned up any evidence against you at all. It sounds like a knee-jerk response from the chief executive and I bet he's regretting it. We should be able to get you an apology and some decent compensation."

Finoula smiled at him in relief. "Just get me my job back, Mr Parsons."

***

Two weeks later, at nine o'clock on a Monday morning, the members of the enquiry met in the boardroom, now the office of Brian Farrell, Chief Executive of St Paul's. There were seven people around the long oak table. Farrell, as chairman, sat in the centre, facing the door. Jimmy Greenhalgh was on his right with Wendy Clarke beside him. Two non-executives from the hospital board sat on the chairman's left, and beyond them, at the end of the table, College Colin and Tony Parsons shuffled their papers.

Farrell began by explaining their terms of reference. "This enquiry has been instigated by the Trust Board. They have asked us to investigate the circumstances of the meningitis outbreak in the spring. We are specifically requested to identify the reasons, if any, for the exceptional mortality and to make recommendations for the management of such outbreaks in the future."

"Hang on a minute!" Tony Parsons interrupted him from the end of the table. "I thought this was an enquiry into the actions of Sister Murphy."

"Her actions may be relevant, certainly. I imagine that's why you're here. But Sister Murphy is not the subject of the enquiry."

"So why did you suspend her?"

Jimmy was pleased to see the chief executive attacked in this way. He could guess what had happened. Farrell had realised that Sister Murphy should never have been suspended on suspicion alone, without evidence against her. It would have been difficult to justify a formal enquiry into a nurse's actions with no proof of malpractice, so the emphasis had been changed.

"She was suspended on Dr Greenhalgh's advice."

"That's not the case; she was suspended by you because I voiced anxieties about the deaths."

"I have a copy here of your letter to Sister Murphy." Tony Parsons read from it: "I'm writing to confirm your suspension on full pay pending an enquiry by the hospital board into the meningitis deaths on Upper South ward in March. She naturally assumed the enquiry was about her."

"Then she was wrong."

Celia Willoughby, one of the two non-executive directors, confirmed that Sister Murphy had not been mentioned when the enquiry had been set up at a hospital board meeting.

There was an embarrassed silence, and Parsons decided to leave it for the moment. The more he pressed, the more Farrell would want to incriminate Sister Murphy to justify his actions. He realised also that her union representatives would normally only attend an enquiry of this type when she was actually being questioned. Their invitation to the whole proceedings was a deliberate concession, an attempt to get their cooperation. Any information they obtained could possibly be to her advantage.

"We'll move on," Farrell said hastily. "Dr Greenhalgh will explain the background to the epidemic."

"It wasn't an epidemic, it was a cluster of cases. We couldn't find any evidence of contact between them."

"I find that extraordinary," Celia said. "It must pass from person to person, so why can't you find contacts?"

"The meningococcus is an odd bug. Thirty per cent of the population carry it in their mouths at some stage, quite harmlessly. It's entirely possible that somebody around this table will cough it out today."

Farrell flinched, and Celia grinned. Jimmy liked her. They had met socially on occasions and he knew her background. Her children had grown up and left home, and she wanted to fill the vacuum by doing something useful. She provided unprejudiced common sense.

"We've had clusters like this in the past," he continued. "They're not that unusual. And we expect people to die. Other bacteria can cause meningitis, the pneumococcus for example, but meningococcal meningitis is the really dangerous one; it's a vicious bacterium when it decides to be."

"What's the normal mortality?" Celia asked.

"Ten to fifteen per cent."

"And this time?"

"They all died."

"And that's why we're here," Farrell said impatiently. "The hospital board is obviously concerned about this high mortality. It may be chance but it's also possible we can learn from it. Dr Greenhalgh will tell us the facts."

"There were six cases," Jimmy said. "They were all admitted in March of this year and all died within forty-eight hours of admission, two on the intensive care unit and the next four on Upper South. The first two were very ill. They had evidence of septicaemia—blood poisoning—with a rash and low blood pressure when they arrived at St Paul's, and they went straight to intensive care. Everything possible was done, entirely by the book, but nobody was surprised when they died. These were the only two of the six who weren't given Penicillin by their GP, and that might have made a difference. The sooner the antibiotic is given the better."

"So their GPs were at fault?" Farrell said.

"Not at all. The early symptoms of meningitis are much like flu, and there was a lot of that about at the time. They did well to recognise meningitis. But once other GPs hear that there are cases around, their threshold for making the diagnosis drops, and if meningitis is even a remote possibility they'll always give the first shot of penicillin at home. The next four patients were all given it before the ambulance arrived."

"But they still died," Celia said.

"Yes, and that's the worrying thing. They weren't particularly ill when they arrived in hospital. They all had the diagnosis confirmed with a lumbar puncture straight away, and high-dose antibiotic was given. They should have had a good chance of survival, but they just didn't seem to respond."

Geoffrey Ayling, the other non-executive director, seated on Celia's left, coughed politely. "Could that be chance? You've said it's a nasty infection."

"It could be, but I've found no record in the literature of a cluster where everybody died."

"So why did it happen here?" said the chief executive impatiently.

"There are three possibilities. The first, and by far the most likely, is that it was just bad luck; a nasty bug. The second is that the antibiotic powder was flawed or polluted in some way. The third possibility is that the penicillin, although prescribed, was never given."

"Explain the last option please," Tony Parsons said quietly.

"I can't, and I'm sure it's nonsense, but we're here to investigate the deaths. We have to consider it."

It was a long morning. Jimmy described the illness of meningitis in detail. Celia was clearly fascinated but Farrell was restless. Jimmy wondered what Geoffrey Ayling made of it all. He was a local farmer only recently appointed to the hospital board.

Eventually, Jimmy returned to the three possibilities. "We should consider first if the patients were just unlucky, or whether perhaps they were infected with a particularly nasty type of meningitis."

Celia asked about the different strains.

"Two infect humans, Type B and Type C."

"Which is worse?"

"Neither, really. They're both potential killers."

"Which strain infected our patients?"

"Both. One of the deaths on ITU was caused by B and one by C. We only grew the bacterium in specimens from one of the Upper South cases, probably because they'd had antibiotics from their GP already and that affects the pick-up rate. It was Type C."

"What about the sensitivities from the ones you did grow?" Tony Parsons asked.

"All sensitive to penicillin."

"So really nothing to support the idea of a new superbug?"

"Nothing definite."

"Let's break for coffee," Farrell said.

***

Thirty minutes later they sat again around the long oak table. Farrell opened the discussion.

"Dr Greenhalgh would like the blame for the deaths to fall sole-ly on the shoulders of the bacteria, but there is no hard evidence to support this. We better look at his second possibility."

"Bacteria don't have shoulders," Jimmy said irritably, "but I agree we have to look beyond the bugs. The second possibility is that there was something wrong with the antibiotic powder."

He described how he had come back to his ward late one night, concerned about the last meningitis patient, and had found Sister Murphy giving the penicillin. He explained how he had checked the dose on an ampoule. It was then that he had seen the scratch on the metal rim of the lid.

"I checked the ward box. There were six ampoules left and they all had the same mark."

"Did you follow it up?"

"Of course I did. Next morning I asked the senior pharmacist, Frances Swynnerton, to look into it."

Frances had been asked to make herself available for the enquiry and was waiting outside. Jimmy invited her to explain what hap-pened next.

"I phoned the medical officer of the drug company. He called back later and confirmed there was a fault in their crimping ma-chine, which had been corrected. Our ampoules were part of the marked batch."

"Could the fault have caused the penicillin to be contaminat-ed?" Geoffrey asked.

"I sent back all the marked ward ampoules for urgent analysis. They contained pure penicillin."

The chief executive smiled at Frances. He admired her crisp ef-ficiency, which he found very attractive. "So much for possibility number two. Thank you for your time."

Frances hesitated. "There is one thing I ought perhaps to men-tion."

Jimmy looked up at her in surprise.

"Of course," Farrell said.

"Yesterday, for completeness, I went back and checked all the drugs issued from pharmacy to Upper South during March. We seem to have supplied a lot more five-millilitre ampoules of sterile water than we did in February."

Jimmy stared at Frances. Celia and Geoffrey looked puzzled, and Tony Parsons and College Colin muttered urgently together at the end of the table.

Farrell looked at the clock. "Lunchtime," he said. "Start again at two p.m."

Jimmy excused himself when coffee and sandwiches were brought into the boardroom, explaining that he had patients to see. He went straight to his office and bleeped Frances.

"You never told me about this!"

"I only thought about checking it yesterday and I didn't get the figures until this morning. It's probably nothing, but I thought I should mention it." She giggled. "Did you see the dreadful Farrell trying to look up my skirt?"

"So was I." Jimmy relaxed. "You don't think it means anything?"

"I doubt it. Would you like to interfere with a witness? Shall I come round to your office?"

"For God's sake," Jimmy said.

***

College Colin and Tony Parsons huddled together in a corner of the boardroom, each with a small plate of sandwiches. Colin had an apple juice and Parsons a black coffee.

"That'll give you indigestion," Colin said.

"St Paul's gives me indigestion," Parsons said. "There's never enough sandwiches here."

"We have a client-orientated performance management ethos," Colin explained incomprehensibly. "Money is scarce."

"I bet your board has a decent lunch. Anyway let's talk about the sterile water. Why would Upper South need many more ampoules in March than they did in February?"

Colin thought. "Most likely is that they had an influx of student nurses on the practical part of their training."

"And they'd use the sterile water to practice injections." Parsons nodded. "Let's hope she had a lot of students that month."

"What if she didn't?"

He looked anxious. "I don't know. I'm wondering what other interpretation might be put on it."

The chief executive sat at the oak boardroom table between Celia and Geoffrey Ayling after they had collected their sandwiches. Wendy Clarke had gone back to her office. Geoffrey noticed that Farrell's plate was piled high.

"It's always the same," he said. "The medics look after themselves."

"Are they really doing that?" Celia said surprised. "I thought this was a very honest analysis of the epidemic."

"Cluster, I think," Geoffrey said ponderously. She looked at him in surprise. "No evidence of a connection between cases." He beamed at her over Farrell's head and winked.

"Cluster, then." Celia smiled back.

"Whatever you want to call it, the point is that the doctors never turn out to be at fault," Farrell said. "They're ultimately responsible, after all. If we'd lost a lorry-load of BBQs when I was in business I would have carried the can."

"I doubt that, somehow," Geoffrey muttered.

A few minutes later, Farrell's secretary phoned and he left the boardroom.

"Can't take to that chap."

Celia agreed. "It's an odd world that puts him in charge of a hospital. Anyway, what do you think so far?"

"It seems that we can't blame the bug for being more virulent, the patients were apparently prescribed the right treatment, and the pharmacist lady has told us there was nothing wrong with the antibiotics on the ward. We're going to have to look at Dr Greenhalgh's third possibility."

"That the penicillin was never given. And that means we'll have to talk to Sister Murphy."

Geoffrey looked across the room at the two representatives from the nursing union. "There's no evidence against her unless something turns up today. We'll have to tread very carefully."

Wendy Clarke, Jimmy and the chief executive returned at two o'clock. After a brief summary of the morning's discussions, Farrell turned to Wendy. "Now we've got to decide if the patients ever got the penicillin. Would you like to tell us what you've discovered?"

"Dr Greenhalgh has already explained that we shouldn't consider the first two patients who died on intensive care. They were seriously ill on admission and their deaths weren't unexpected. The next four went to Upper South."

"I believe you've got two medical wards," Celia interrupted. "Why did they all go to Upper South?"

"Only the luck of the draw. The two wards admit medical emergencies on alternate days. It was just chance that Sister Murphy's ward was on take when all four were admitted to hospital."

Tony Parsons looked up sharply. "I hadn't realised we were discussing her"

Wendy looked to the chief executive for guidance.

"This enquiry wasn't set up specifically to examine her actions," Farrell said irritably. "I've already explained that. But we're all aware that she is supposed to have given the injections. We can hardly avoid talking about her!"

Wendy continued, "The cases were admitted to Upper South over a four-week period. The first was a twenty-year-old female student from the local technical college. Twelve days after her death, a twenty-two-year-old man died on the ward. The next patient was admitted six days later. She was eighteen. A week after she died, the last one came in, a painter and decorator in his mid-twenties. They all died within three days of admission."

"All so young!" Celia said.

"It tends to be a disease of young people," Jimmy said.

"And they all died so quickly!"

"I've known people die within twenty-four hours of first feeling ill."

Geoffrey Ayling stirred heavily in his chair. "What happened in the days before antibiotics? Did they all die quickly? Did anybody survive?"

"I don't know for sure, but I can't believe that anyone could have survived once the signs of meningitis or septicaemia were present, at least not without serious brain damage."

"How long, would you guess?"

"Three to four days at best."

"So if our four patients received no penicillin in hospital and if they'd been ill for a day at home first, they just about died on time. Is that right?"

Jimmy agreed.

Wendy continued. "I've gone back through the patients' notes and the ward records, checking to see who actually gave the injections." She looked apologetically at Tony Parsons. "Most of the time it was Finoula Murphy."

"But not all of the time?"

"No. She worked a shift system when the first two patients were on the ward, either seven thirty a.m. to four thirty p.m., or one thirty p.m. to nine thirty p.m. She changed shift every two days."

"All right," Parsons said. "So she was only around for nine hours each day. The patients were getting penicillin six hourly. At the most she could only have given half the injections?"

"At St Paul's we normally give six-hourly drugs at six in the morning, midday, six in the evening and midnight."

Celia scribbled on her pad. "In that case, she would only have been present on the ward for one of the injections!"

"In theory, yes. But often when she had very sick patients, she would come into work early and leave late. She did that with the first two meningitis patients."

Celia looked up. "If she started the early shift at six and worked for twelve hours, she could have given three of the injections."

"And if she started the late shift at midday and finished at midnight, she could also only have given three," Geoffrey calculated.

"So did she?" Celia asked.

"Yes. She personally gave three injections each day to the first two meningitis patients."

"Would one proper dose of penicillin each day be enough to fight the infection?"

"I doubt it," Jimmy said.

There was a brief silence in the boardroom, then Tony Parsons spoke. "This proves nothing, of course, except that Sister Murphy is a dedicated nurse. You wouldn't find the modern generation working a twelve-hour day they weren't paid for!" He glanced at College Colin, who reluctantly agreed.

"You've only mentioned the first two patients," Geoffrey Ayling said to Wendy. "What about the third and fourth?"

Wendy told them what Jimmy already knew. She explained how Sister Murphy had cancelled her leave after the second death, changed herself from shift work onto day duty, instructed the houseman to alter the time of the last dose from midnight to 11 p.m. and visited the ward briefly at 6 a.m. and 11 p.m. to give the first and last injections.

Geoffrey and Celia stared at her. "You mean she contrived things so she could give all the injections herself?" Celia said.

Farrell nodded. "Exactly. Pretty damning stuff if you ask me!"

"Pretty damning or pretty impressive," Tony Parsons said angrily. "Depends where you start from. It wasn't at all unusual when I practiced nursing for a dedicated sister to come back to the ward after hours if she was worried about a patient." He looked at Wendy. "You must have asked her why she did it?"

"She said she didn't trust the new generation of nurses: 'Too much theory in their training and not enough practical' were her actual words."

Parsons felt College Colin stiffen beside him and put a hand on his arm.

"You're saying she didn't believe that her own nurses were competent enough to give intravenous injections!" Geoffrey stared at Wendy. "Is that reasonable?"

"She wouldn't have meant it quite as strongly as that," Wendy said. "She was only saying that with really sick patients she wanted to be sure everything had been done correctly."

"Can nurses in training give intravenous injections?" Celia asked.

"No, only qualified staff are allowed to, and even then they have to get the hospital certificate first."

"Do you believe she had cause to be worried that the penicillin wouldn't be given correctly?" Geoffrey asked Wendy directly.

"No," she said unhappily. "I don't believe she had."

Farrell took charge. "All right." He glanced briefly at Tony Parsons. "We've established that Sister Murphy manipulated things so that she gave most of the penicillin injections to the four patients who died. Possibly that was just misguided dedication on her part, but we must satisfy ourselves that she actually injected the antibiotic into the patients."

Jimmy Greenhalgh interrupted. "Let's all be clear what we're talking about. I'm sure everybody remembers the Beverley Allitt case. She was the paediatric nurse who interfered with the treatment of thirteen children, actually killing four of them. It was some months before her activities were even suspected, and now she's in prison for life. There have been two similar incidents in the States, but the Allitt case is the only time it's happened in this country, as far as we know."

"Do you mean it might have happened elsewhere and not been discovered?" Geoffrey asked.

"Who knows? But once the unthinkable's occurred, it's part of human experience. You have to believe it could happen again. At least you have to be aware that it might."

Tony Parsons looked at Wendy. "Have you any evidence that Sister Murphy didn't give the injections?"

"None."

"All right, then; put it another way. Have you any evidence that she did?" Geoffrey said.

"Only that her signature is in the prescription chart as having given them."

"Could you explain that, please?" Celia asked.

"Hospitals vary in this, but at St Paul's we have a system where two nurses have to sign the prescription sheet when an intravenous injection is given. They check the dose of the drug together, draw it up into a syringe, using sterile water to dissolve the powder if necessary, and then go together to the bedside. They check they have the right patient by looking at his identity bracelet and one of them gives the injection into an intravenous cannula already placed in a vein by the houseman. She signs as having given the drug, and the other nurse signs as having checked the dose."

Geoffrey and Celia stared at her for a moment. "So what's the problem?" Geoffrey asked. "Either the second nurse saw her give the injection or she didn't."

Wendy sighed. "None of the nurses who signed with Sister Murphy can actually remember her giving the injections."

"None of them!"

"No," Wendy said.

Farrell glared at Tony Parsons. "Still think I was wrong to suspend your girl?"

Parsons ignored him. "Now hold on a minute," he said to Wendy. "All this was some time ago. It's not surprising that hard-pressed nurses can't remember every injection."

"But surely they wouldn't forget them all," Celia said. "These were young patients dying unexpectedly!"

"I've already discussed this with Mrs Clarke," Farrell said, "and there's a perfectly simple explanation why nobody can remember

Sister Murphy giving the injections." He looked around the table, savouring the suspense.

"Well, go on, man!" Geoffrey said impatiently.

"Nobody can remember because she always insisted on being alone when she gave them."

Celia stared at him. "Seriously?"

Wendy answered. "We can't say that for certain, but most of the nurses who signed with her can remember being told not to bother to come, and none of them can remember going with her."

Thoughtful silences were becoming a feature of the enquiry.

Eventually, Geoffrey spoke. "You've told us it's policy at St Paul's for two nurses to be at the bedside when an intravenous injection is given. Is that a legal requirement?"

"Sister Murphy did nothing illegal," Tony Parsons said. "Once a nurse is qualified, she's entitled to give any drug on her own. It doesn't even have to be checked by another nurse. Hospital policies vary, and St Paul's is unusually strict. Most insist that two nurses check the drug when it's drawn up, but only a few require two nurses to go to the bedside."

"Nevertheless, she works at St Paul's," Farrell said impatiently, "and she ignored hospital policy. We can sack her for that alone."

"If you do that you'll have to sack most of your senior nurses," Wendy said quietly. She glanced at College Colin but thought better of asking him for his support. "It's not unusual for ward sisters to give an intravenous injection on their own, especially when the ward is busy."

"Christ!" Farrell had had enough. "I don't believe this. We're worried that one of the nurses is murdering patients but we won't admit it to each other. We discover that our main suspect has deliberately changed rotas and cancelled her holiday so she can give all the injections herself, and then we find that she's used her authority to insist that nobody watch her. But whenever we turn up more damning evidence, you and Parsons say it's probably OK."

Jimmy had been silent for some time. "We need facts," he said. "Circumstantial evidence is not enough."

***

Sister Murphy had been asked to attend the enquiry in the afternoon. She arrived promptly at two o'clock. Eileen Kenny came with her, and they waited anxiously in the anteroom.

Eileen looked sadly at the glossy magazines on the table. "You read the Hospital Manager's Yearbook, and I'll take Client Services in the Year 2000."

Farrell walked through, then Jimmy Greenhalgh came in and went through to the boardroom. Sister Murphy ignored him.

Wendy Clarke rushed in a few minutes later. She smiled sympathetically at Finoula. "Don't get upset. And don't get cross! Tony Parsons will look after you."

An hour and a half later, she came out of the boardroom. "They're ready for you now. Remember what I said."

Eileen squeezed Finoula's hand. "I'll wait here for you."

Finoula sat in an upright chair in front of the boardroom table, and Wendy introduced her to the members of the enquiry. The non-executive directors and Tony Parsons smiled encouragingly, but College Colin stared at the table. Farrell watched her carefully, contrasting unfavourably the small, dark, resentful woman with the tall, blonde, self-assured pharmacist of the morning.

He won't be looking up Sister Murphy's skirt, Jimmy thought to himself.

"And of course you know Dr Greenhalgh," Wendy finished.

"We've worked together for fifteen years," Jimmy said, but she ignored him.

Farrell began by explaining carefully the remit of the enquiry. "We want to know if we can learn from the deaths. Perhaps you can help us."

She stared at him. "I don't understand. Two months ago you wrote to me saying I was suspended pending this enquiry."

"We would be grateful for your expert help," Farrell said lamely.

"So presumably you've suspended all the other witnesses?"

Tony Parsons stepped in. "The chief executive has made it quite clear to us that this is an enquiry into the deaths, not an enquiry into you. Of course, when this is over, the Royal College of Nursing will want to discuss your suspension with him."

They had already agreed that Wendy should begin the questioning. She started by summarising the morning's discussion. "We don't feel there was anything unusual about the bacteria, and we've heard that the penicillin was checked by the manufacturer, who found nothing wrong with it. We want to be sure that the patients actually got the antibiotics prescribed for them. We understand that you arranged things so you gave most of the injections yourself. Could you explain to us why you did that?"

"I thought it safest to do it myself."

Geoffrey leant forward. "Why didn't you think it was safe to let the other nurses do it?"

She looked at him. He seemed kind, and she relaxed slightly. "I'm sure it sounds daft to you. I'm not saying they're all useless, but students are taught these days in a way that makes them pretty incompetent when they come on the wards."

"Why's that?"

"The people at the top seem to want to pretend that nursing is an intellectual profession rather than a practical one. They fill the students' heads with sociology and management claptrap and forget to teach them how to make a bed." She was aware that the panel was watching her intently.

"Why do you think it's like that?" Geoffrey asked.

Out of the corner of her eye, she could see College Colin glaring at her. "Because nurses who make a career out of it and work their way to the top are often frustrated doctors. They're the ones who do the damage by trying to pretend that nursing is something it isn't."

"That's ridiculous!" College Colin regretted his outburst as soon as he'd made it, but Farrell seized the opportunity.

"Go on."

Tony Parsons stepped in. "I'm sure Mr Smythe didn't mean to interrupt."

"Then I'd like him to tell us that himself."

Colin was fed up. He couldn't believe that Sister Murphy was another Beverley Allitt, but Tony Parsons and Wendy were persuading the panel that her experience entitled her to ignore hospital guidelines on nursing practice, many of which he had written himself. He was heavily involved with teaching student nurses and an enthusiastic supporter of the modern syllabus.

"Sister Murphy is well known for her reactionary views."

"You don't agree with them?" Farrell said.

Tony Parsons spoke before Colin could reply. "There are bound to be different shades of opinion in any profession. Surely that's healthy?"

Farrell continued to speak directly to Colin. "Are you saying that Sister Murphy's refusal to move with the times makes her unsafe?"

"I didn't hear him say anything of the sort," Geoffrey interjected smoothly. He smiled sympathetically at Finoula. "You were telling us why you felt you had to give the injections yourself."

She sensed an ally. "It was probably unnecessary, I realise that, but I've seen patients die with meningitis before and I know how dangerous it is. I live just around the corner, and it's no hardship to come in at odd hours."

Geoffrey nodded. "We've heard that hospital guidelines recommend two nurses being present when the injection is given."

Finoula snorted. "That wouldn't surprise me."

Farrell butted in. "Do you mean you're not aware of hospital policy?"

She looked at him calmly. "The world you managers live in is completely different from the real world on the wards. If we took notice of every bit of paper you sent round, St Paul's would grind to a halt."

Farrell was speechless. Jimmy fiddled with his papers, trying hard not to laugh, and Tony Parsons raised his eyes to the ceiling.

Celia spoke next. She asked Finoula why she had altered her annual leave, and she explained that she'd had nothing special planned and wanted to see the epidemic out.

"Cluster," Geoffrey muttered.

Farrell was increasingly frustrated. He didn't know if she had withheld the penicillin or not, but he wasn't going to carry the can if the enquiry cleared her and it subsequently transpired that she had. He wanted rid of her.

"Tell us about the sterile water," he said, watching her closely.

She stared at him, but Tony Parsons spoke first. "Sister Murphy hasn't heard about the sterile water. What do you expect her to say?"

"Of course. I'll explain. This morning we heard from Mrs Swynnerton, the hospital pharmacist, that Upper South ordered an excessive amount of sterile water in March."

"Sterile water?"

The panel waited until eventually Celia prompted her. "What would you normally use sterile water for?"

"Making up drugs, I suppose. Dissolving the powder in ampoules."

"Why would you have needed so much in March?"

"It's news to me, but the meningitis cases would have needed a lot to dissolve the penicillin. That's presumably the reason."

"Would you use sterile water for anything else?"

Finoula thought for a moment, and Geoffrey felt she was flustered.

"The housemen use it sometimes to flush through an intravenous cannula which is blocked, but normally they'd use saline."

"Anything else? You got through an awful lot of it!"

She was silent.

"Would you use it for teaching?" Tony Parsons prompted.

"Oh come on!" Farrell said angrily "Sister Murphy can answer for herself."

She smiled at Parsons, relieved. "Of course we do! The students use it to practise drawing fluids from an ampoule into a syringe. Several students get through a lot of sterile water."

"And you had a lot of students on Upper South in March?"

"I can't remember exactly, but we must have done."

Farrell looked at Wendy, who in turn looked apologetically at Finoula. "I've checked with the School of Nursing. March was a busy time for them and most of the students were on lecture courses. Very few were seconded to the wards."

"How many to Upper South" Farrell asked.

"None," Wendy said.

I don't believe this is happening! Geoffrey thought to himself. He smiled at Sister Murphy. "So it wasn't the students. What else would you use it for?"

She was silent

"Wouldn't you have noticed the extra demand?"

"We don't record it."

"Then how do you know when you need more from the pharmacy?"

"There's a box, a pharmacy box on the ward. When we finish a carton of a stock item like sterile water, we throw it in the box. Next day the pharmacy replaces it."

"They have a record and you don't?"

She nodded.

"If it wasn't used for flushing drips or teaching students to give injections, it must have been used for dissolving drugs," Farrell said. "Is that correct?"

"I suppose so."

He looked at Wendy. "Have you found out how much they should have needed in March for intravenous drugs?"

"Mrs Swynnerton had done that already. I checked with her during the lunch break."

"And?"

"Apart from the meningitis cases, March was a fairly normal month on Upper South. She worked out that the meningitis cases should have doubled the amount usually required."

"And how much did they actually get through?"

"Three times as much."

Sister Murphy had no explanation for the discrepancy. She seemed to consider it an irrelevance, and they couldn't pin her down. Eventually they gave up.

"Thank you very much," Farrell said.

"Is that it?"

"We're grateful for your help."

"When can I go back to work?"

"Sister Clarke will be in touch."

***

Finoula and Eileen Kenny walked home.

"Well come on," Eileen said. "What did they say?"

"I can't remember all of it. A lot of stuff about sterile water."

Eileen stopped walking and stared at her. "Sterile water!"

"Apparently we used a lot in March."

"So what?"

"I don't know. It seemed to be important."

***

The panel sat in awkward silence after she had gone.

Celia turned to Jimmy. "I'm lost. Is she crazy or is it all coincidence?"

He sipped his tea, trying to hide that his hand was shaking. "When I came onto the ward that night, she was standing behind the nurses' desk drawing up the drug. I watched her do it and followed her to the patient, so I know she gave the antibiotic."

"She didn't know you were coming back?"

"No. I hadn't told her I'd be back."

"Had she begun to draw up the penicillin before you arrived?"

He thought. "She had the ampoules ready, the ones with the marks on the lids, so presumably she was going to draw it up. She was in full view of the other nurses, after all. The intravenous drugs are made up on the work surface just behind the nurses' station."

"So if you hadn't come, she'd have set off down the ward to the patient with a syringe full of penicillin?" Geoffrey said.

"Could she just have squirted it down the sink?" Celia asked.

He shook his head. "The patients were conscious, to begin with at least. They'd have noticed if their medication was missed. She'd have had to give them something."

"Something?" Farrell said. "What do you mean by something? Do you mean she might have given sterile water?"

Nobody spoke for a while.

It was Geoffrey who broke the silence. "So she draws up the penicillin and sets off down the ward to the patient. When nobody can see her, she swaps the antibiotic syringe for one containing only sterile water that she's drawn up already." He looked at Wendy. "Where would she conceal it?"

"Sisters' dresses have big, loose pockets. It wouldn't be a problem."

"It would explain the extra sterile water almost exactly," Farrell said.

Parsons stood up. "I've listened to this long enough. No evidence has been produced against Sister Murphy at all, but we've spun a web of dreadful fantasies around the conscientious behaviour of a dedicated sister. The chief executive suspended her impulsively without evidence, and I must insist now that she is reinstated with a clean record, a proper apology and appropriate compensation."

"No, wait," Geoffrey said. "We're getting ahead of ourselves here. There appear to be too many coincidences to ignore, but then again, it seems they could reasonably be interpreted either way. Let's just talk through the consequences of whatever decision we make."

"Go ahead," Farrell said reluctantly.

"If we do decide she *is* guilty, the first thing we must do is involve the police. I'm sure we're all agreed on that. There will be no question of secrecy once we've done that, not with a story like this. It will be in the national papers even while the police are still investigating, and Sister Murphy will be named. Her life will be ruined and she will never nurse again, whether she is charged or not. But what evidence are they going to find against her that we haven't? It's all circumstantial."

"Oh come on!" Farrell said. "Are you really saying that if we think she's guilty we can do nothing about it? That's ridiculous."

"I'm saying we need more than we have at the moment before we can involve the police. She's our employee; we have a responsibility towards her. We can't just destroy her without very good reason, and I don't believe we have that reason."

"I don't really understand why her approach to nursing practice should be so different to yours." Celia smiled at College Colin.

"Let me explain that," Parsons said before his colleague could answer. "It's all to do with Project 2000. This was first mooted in 1986 as a program for altering the way nurses were taught. Traditionally, most hospitals, even quite small ones, had their own nursing schools and their own nurse tutors. From the moment a nurse entered the school, she was seen as a part of the nursing workforce and her training would involve long spells on the wards learning the practicalities of nursing, interspersed with shorter spells in the school attending lectures and demonstrations. Nursing was understood to be a practical profession, not an academic one. Project 2000 wants to change this, with the practical side of nurse education becoming secondary to the academic one, and eventually nurse education becoming centred in universities. It will be a while before this happens, if it ever does, but the concept is gaining momentum and is already reflected in the way nurses are taught. Many older nurses, like Sister Murphy, see no need for this and, rightly or wrongly, are convinced that newly qualified nurses lack basic nursing skills."

Farrell was getting restless. "Let's stick to the point. What are we going to do about Sister Murphy? Pretend none of this ever happened?"

"That's what we need to discuss," Geoffrey said. "But surely first we need to know what we all think. Why don't you ask us individually?"

"Off the record," Parsons insisted.

"OK," Farrell said. "Off the record: *innocent* or *guilty*."

"Or *don't know*," Celia said. "I can't believe I'm the only one who's uncertain."

"All right, *innocent, guilty* or *don't know*."

He went round the table.

There were four "don't knows": Wendy Clarke, Jimmy Greenhalgh, Celia Willoughby and Geoffrey Ayling. There were two "innocents": Tony Parsons and Colin Smythe. Only Farrell voted "guilty".

"'*Don't know*' means just that," Farrell pointed out. "She might or might not be guilty. Only two of the seven us are convinced she didn't do it. If we can't fire her, we've got to watch her obsessively. Is there any workable way we can stop her giving intravenous injections if she continues as a sister?"

"Giving all the injections herself and insisting she be unobserved was irresponsible, and of course she completely ignored hospital guidelines," Wendy said. "She should be disciplined for that alone. I suppose we could stop her giving intravenous injections on those grounds."

"How do you think she'd respond to that?"

"She'd be humiliated."

"Would she resign?" Farrell said hopefully.

"I don't think she would want to. She's just had her fifty-ninth birthday. I know she had planned to retire at sixty with her full pension entitlement."

"Careful observation, then, but hopefully not for more than a year. How do we organise that? And don't forget this enquiry was instigated by the Trust Board. We have to report to them."

Parsons said, "I'll only go along with this if her anonymity is guaranteed. That won't happen if she's mentioned in the report to the board."

Celia looked at Geoffrey. "Her name was never mentioned at board meetings, was it, Geoffrey?" She glanced at her notes. "We were only asked to identify reasons for the high mortality, if any, and make recommendations for the management of similar clusters in the future."

Jimmy spoke. "Wendy and I can keep an eye on her."

"We need something more formal than that," Farrell said. "There has to be documentation that we are taking this very seriously. You need to meet to discuss her on a regular basis—let's say monthly—and keep minutes of your meetings, which you send to me. And surely you'd want input from the pharmacy? I suggest we ask Mrs Swynnerton to join you. Which means she'll have to know what all this is about. Is everybody happy with that?"

There was no dissent.

CHAPTER ELEVEN

Geoffrey Ayling loved his farm and was happiest when sitting behind the wheel of a tractor for hours on end. He collapsed in an armchair on an autumn evening after a long day ploughing while Fiona poured gin and tonic, and his father's portrait above the fireplace looked down with approval on his dusty and exhausted son. The 3000-acre farm had been in Geoffrey's family for three generations. He was an only child, schooled at Gresham's with the sons of Norfolk farmers, and his future had never been in doubt. His father had retired ten years before, giving the big house to Geoffrey and Fiona and moving with Geoffrey's mother to a smaller house on the farm, although he still phoned Geoffrey most days with advice, some of it welcome. They had two children, a boy and a girl, both at Gresham's. The boy seemed interested in farming, but of course it was early days.

Geoffrey was a large man, well over six foot, heavily built and obviously strong. He kept his fair hair short. His face was weathered and there were deep laughter wrinkles beside his brown eyes. His hands, always dirt-engrained, were enormous. He was well liked in Norfolk farming circles, sitting on several local committees, and nobody was surprised when he joined the board at St Paul's as a non-executive director.

"Food's ready," Fiona said. "It'll keep as long as you like. Go and relax in the bath for half an hour."

"Any messages?"

"There was one." Fiona frowned. "A sister from your hospital. She wants you to call her back."

He sat up straight. "Sister Murphy?"

She looked at the pad by the phone. "That's her."

"How did she sound?"

"Anxious, maybe a bit agitated. Who is she, Geoffrey?"

"Just one of the senior nurses."

In the two weeks since the enquiry, he had never discussed Sister Murphy at home or elsewhere. Tony Parsons had been adamant about that, and Geoffrey had no doubt that he would seek expensive compensation for her suspension if there was any leak.

"She wants to meet you. She left her phone number." Fiona gave him his drink. He smiled gratefully and pulled her down for a kiss.

He called Sister Murphy after supper.

"I'd like to talk to you," she said, her soft Irish brogue bringing the day in the boardroom back into sharp focus.

"What about?"

"It's to do with the enquiry."

"Can't you tell me on the phone?"

"I'd rather come to your house."

He was nervous. "Shouldn't you discuss it with Wendy Clarke?"

"I'd sooner talk to you."

He thought for a moment. "I'd like Celia Willoughby to be here as well. Would you mind that?"

"Yes, I would." She sounded irritated. "I don't want another mini enquiry; I just want to discuss something. Can I come tomorrow evening? I know where you live."

Reluctantly, Geoffrey agreed.

The next day, he came in from the fields at six o'clock to find her already there.

"She's in the study," Fiona said. "Not exactly a bundle of fun, is she? Would you like a drink first?"

"Better not. I might need a clear head."

She watched him curiously as he closed the door.

It was a working room, opening directly through a back door to a small porch which led to the yard outside the house, and like many farm offices it was a complete mess. Dusty, unread journals were piled on a corner of the desk, and the ink-stained blotting pad in the centre was just visible under a pile of bills. Fiona had seated Sister Murphy in a comfortable, scuffed leather armchair, and she jumped up when Geoffrey came in, twisting her hands nervously in front of her. Normally he would have sat at his desk, but he wanted her to relax and so took the second armchair with broken springs, the one reserved for salesmen he didn't really want to see. They shook hands and he smiled as they both sat down.

"How can I help?"

She was silent for a few moments and then looked directly at him for the first time. "I thought you understood what I was saying at the enquiry."

"About what, exactly?"

"About why I wanted to give the injections myself."

Geoffrey remembered her comments on modern nursing training and thought also about the show of hands at the end of the day. He said nothing.

"I thought you understood I'd done nothing wrong, but I had the feeling some of the others only let me off because they couldn't prove anything against me."

"Is that why you've come to see me?"

She was silent for a moment, gathering her thoughts, while Geoffrey waited patiently, uncomfortably aware of the sharp end of a spring sticking into his thigh.

"There was a lot of talk at the enquiry about sterile water. Why were you all so interested in how much we used on Upper South?"

"We wanted all the information we could get. Mrs Swynnerton said that Upper South had used a lot of sterile water that month. She'd noticed it in the pharmacy records."

"So you didn't hear about it until the day of the enquiry?"

He thought back. "No, I'm sure we didn't. She mentioned it in passing just before we broke for lunch."

"In passing?"

"Yes, almost as an afterthought. She didn't think it was important."

"Did you all think it was important?"

"It was a confidential enquiry," Geoffrey said gently. "You can't expect me to discuss it with you."

Finoula sighed. "I talked to my friend Eileen Kenny about it. She's a sister on the surgical ward. She couldn't work out either why we'd use so much if we didn't have students. It wasn't a busy month apart from the meningitis cases. We thought pharmacy must have made a mistake."

"I don't think so. We asked Mrs Swynnerton to check her records again after the enquiry. There wasn't any doubt."

"And then the other day I realised suddenly that if we'd really used a lot of sterile water we must have used a lot more syringes."

"How do you mean?"

"We only draw sterile water from five-millilitre ampoules into syringes. The quantity is too small for anything else. So if we used a lot more ampoules, we should have used a lot more syringes."

"Do you know how many syringes you got through?" he asked unwillingly, not sure what answer he wanted to hear.

"We don't record that on the ward. It wouldn't be practical because we use so many. Every two weeks somebody from supplies comes up to see what we've got left."

"They replace the ones you've used?"

"They stock us up again, back to the same level."

"And they keep a record?"

She lifted a shapeless black handbag onto her lap and rummaged through it, eventually finding a thin, curled sheaf of photocopied paper, which she handed to him. "They gave me this. It's a record of the ward supplies for January, February, March and April. The syringes are in there. I've underlined them."

He studied the order sheets, deliberately taking his time. She had marked the relevant bits with a fluorescent yellow pen, and he could see at once that Upper South had used roughly the same number of syringes each month, and certainly no more than usual in March. He thought hard while he pretended to work through the sheets.

"It's pretty obvious, isn't it?" she said impatiently. "We didn't use any more syringes."

"I can see that. So what *did* you do with the extra sterile water?"

"*I don't know*," Finoula said fiercely. "Are you sure the pharmacy records are accurate?"

Next morning he phoned Jimmy Greenhalgh's secretary and arranged to meet him in his office that afternoon.

"So how did you leave it?" Jimmy said.

"I said I'd talk to you." Geoffrey smiled. "She just snorted. I don't think you're her favourite person."

"She blames me for the enquiry."

"The records from supplies are genuine. Wendy Clarke checked that for me. Do you think Frances Swynnerton might have muddled Upper South's order with another ward?"

"No. She's checked and double checked. We asked her to do that after the enquiry. I suppose if Sister Murphy *was* going to inject patients with sterile water, she'd hardly order more syringes to do it. She could stockpile them over several months and it wouldn't be obvious from the supplies records, or she could buy them herself. I agree it's odd, but I don't think it gets us anywhere."

PART THREE:

MAY 1996

SIX MONTHS AFTER JIMMY'S DEATH

CHAPTER TWELVE

The murder investigation had got nowhere; no leads, no witnesses, no serious suspects. Suicide had been quickly ruled out. The police had interviewed almost everybody at the hospital, and those who knew Jimmy well could not believe he would take his own life. His behaviour up to the day of his death had been completely normal. He *could* have put the handcuffs key in the hole in the superstructure of the wreck and shackled himself to a rail, snapping the cuffs shut. He *might* have put the key in the hole to stop himself changing his mind. But he could hardly have caused the deep gash to his face and broken his own nose.

How did he get out to the wreck? If he'd gone there to meet somebody, he would have dressed appropriately for a very cold November afternoon on a North Sea beach, but he'd been wearing a lightweight suit as the hospital was always overheated in the winter. Almost certainly he was taken there, presumably against his will, but it would surely have needed more than one man to do this. If the blow to his face had happened before setting out for the wreck, he might have been unable to resist, but then he would have had to be dragged or carried. If he was struck at the wreck, perhaps to silence him, he must have struggled all the way there. Somebody must have seen something.

Low tide on the afternoon of the day he went missing was at 2.30 p.m. The outgoing tide would have exposed the wreck approximately two hours before, at 12.30 p.m., and the incoming tide would have reached it again two hours after low water, at 4.30 p.m. He must therefore have been taken to the wreck between 12.30 and 4.30 p.m. In late November, light was already fading at 4 p.m., so there were at least three and a half hours when somebody could have seen something unusual, but nobody came forward. The predictable tabloid headline, *"TOP DOC TOPPED"*, had produced no helpful information.

Hicks had returned to the beach with two colleagues the day after the post-mortem. The two officers had walked out to the *Jura* together while he watched from the dunes. In the dull grey conditions, they were just visible at the wreck, but it was impossible to see what they were doing there. In fact, the few people on the huge beach were visible only as dark silhouettes unless they were very close.

After 4 p.m., the beach would have been in darkness and it would have been very dangerous to walk near the wreck or to drive a four-wheel truck across the sands. There was a links golf course beside the beach, and the clubhouse looked directly out over the sands. There had been a long lunch party there, but nobody recollected seeing lights on the beach after dark.

Jimmy's car was found parked legally in a back street in Burnham Castle, five miles from Massingham Beach. It was locked and undamaged. There was no sign of a struggle inside. The only fingerprints were those of Jimmy and his wife. Nobody in the village remembered the car being parked.

Jimmy's wife Angela's shocked response when Hicks brought the news of his death had been totally convincing, but anyhow she had an alibi for the afternoon; a friend confirmed that they had been early Christmas shopping together in Holt.

Two names had surfaced during the interviews of hospital staff, Sister Finoula Murphy and Frances Swynnerton. There had been a hospital enquiry into Sister Murphy's practice. The details were confidential and Hicks didn't press when he understood that nothing definite had been found against her. He was told, however, that

Jimmy Greenhalgh had been one of her "accusers". He interviewed her in the house that she shared with her friend Eileen Kenny. He noted how the space had been divided between them and that they were joint owners of the property. She told how Dr Greenhalgh had been shocked when a patient on his ward round had collapsed and died in front of him, and how he had walked straight off the ward, leaving his registrar to finish the round, and how she never saw him again. She was on day duty for the rest of that day and so had an alibi, but just looking at the short, dark, distressed nurse, he had no problem eliminating her as a suspect.

He wasn't sure what to make of Frances Swynnerton. She had been spotted with Jimmy regularly during the summer, going to and from his boat, but they hadn't been seen together since the sailing season ended in mid-September. Were they having an affair? His enquiries revealed nothing to suggest this and no evidence for it. He interviewed Frances himself in her cottage with a female colleague three days after the body was found. She was obviously shaken but tried to be helpful. She explained how Jimmy was often short of a crew. She had been pleased to help out and they had got on well together. Their paths didn't cross in the hospital, and she never saw him otherwise. She had been working the day he went missing. Her role as senior pharmacist involved visiting the wards most afternoons. Her deputy had had a meeting with her that morning in the pharmacy, but nobody could remember seeing her that afternoon, in the pharmacy or on the wards. Hicks asked the same question for the day before and the day after Jimmy went missing and got the same response, and he could understand how a short visit from a white-coated person to a busy ward in a busy hospital might well go unnoticed or unremembered.

The police desperately needed a break, but none was forthcoming.

Until, a few weeks later, Sister Murphy died.

CHAPTER THIRTEEN

Jimmy Greenhalgh's consultant post was advertised in the *British Medical Journal* a month after his death. Six candidates were shortlisted for interview, and Simon Spence, a senior registrar at St Joseph's Hospital in London, was appointed. Shortly after his arrival Angus Wilson, the pathologist, invited Simon and his wife Sally to dinner to welcome them to Norfolk.

"This must be it," Simon said, turning through a white-barred gate into a drive lined with rhododendrons.

Angus lived in a Victorian rectory beside the village church. He had heard the scrunch of gravel and was opening the front door as they parked.

"Would you like a look around?" he offered. "The others haven't arrived yet."

He was proud of his garden, which looked well in the lengthening shadows of the summer evening. They strolled across the lawn to the wide herbaceous border against the south-facing wall and turned to look back at the house. He told them that big old rectories in East Anglia had cost next to nothing when he was appointed to St Paul's a quarter of a century ago. Nobody wanted the bother and expense of maintaining them. Sally breathed the scent of honeysuckle and philadelphus and stared enviously, thinking of their detached modern house with its small garden.

Two cars had drawn up, and Angus led them back to meet his other guests. He had invited Tom and Caroline Easter in case the Spences were hard work.

"Hello Angus," said Caroline, kissing him. "He's my favour-ite pathologist," she told Simon. "I'm going to insist he does my post-mortem. You must be Simon Spence"

Caroline chatted easily to Sally while Angus introduced Simon to Tom Easter, a local general practitioner and an old friend.

"You'll be happy here," Tom said. "We love our part of the world."

They were joined by the driver of the second car. Simon watched her with interest as she kissed Angus on both cheeks. He had seen her somewhere before, a tall, attractive blonde. She had come alone.

"I'm Frances Swynnerton," she said before Angus could intro-duce her. "You don't know me but I've heard all about you."

She explained that she was the senior hospital pharmacist, and he remembered now that he had seen her on the wards in her white coat, checking the drug trolley and looking through prescription sheets.

Angus led them through a vast dark hall into the biggest draw-ing room Sally had ever seen outside a stately home. Heavy brown wooden beams arched from high walls to the ceiling, nearly out of sight as the evening darkened. Tall stone windows framed a view of the herbaceous border and the church beyond. Bright rugs on the floor and buttermilk paint on the walls struggled with only partial success to dispel the gloom. Although it was May, Angus had lit a log fire in the grate, which roared and crackled enthusiastically, emitting no detectable heat.

"I love owning this room, but we hardly ever come into it," he told them. "Far too cold. We used it on Christmas Day until the relatives refused to come and visit us again. When the children were young, the hamsters escaped and we found them in here several weeks later, frozen solid."

Tom helped with the drinks while the Spences talked to Frances by the window.

"Even the tiniest village in Norfolk has a church," she said. "This parish can't have had more than a thousand souls, but it had a vicar all to itself and he was able to support himself and his family in this house. Gives you a feel for how the Church has tumbled."

"I expect he had a private income."

Frances smiled. "Nowadays only doctors can afford houses like this."

"This one can't," Sally said. "I wish he could."

Frances looked at her curiously. "Haven't you found somewhere nice to live?"

"Oh it's all right, small and modern. Not really what we'd hoped for."

"We arrived on the wrong side of the boom," Simon explained. "What about you?"

Frances was describing her rented cottage on the coast when Tom bustled up with the drinks. "Gin and tonic for you, and for you, I think, and gin and tonic for you."

Sally, who had asked for an orange juice, thanked him and sipped nervously at a tumbler of gin with ice and lemon but no obvious tonic.

Frances smiled sympathetically. "I asked for a martini, not a pint of paint stripper. Tom is a better GP than a barman."

"I expect he's like all doctors," Sally said. "Convinced he knows what's best for you."

Frances pointed to a dissolute-looking rubber plant lurking unsteadily in a dark corner. "We usually pour them in there."

Sally laughed, beginning to relax.

Two women had entered the room while they were talking. Simon recognised Mary Wilson, Angus' wife, but not the other. She was short and slightly chubby with a round, pleasant, comfortable face. Her thinning hair was completely white.

"That's Angela Greenhalgh, your predecessor's widow."

Simon watched her with interest. He was aware of the details of Jimmy Greenhalgh's death, handcuffed to the wreck until the tide had come in and drowned him. Although it had happened six months ago, the police investigation had apparently got nowhere.

At the inquest, the coroner had recorded a verdict of *"unnatural death by person or persons unknown"*.

Angus bought Angela over to the window and introduced her. She held Simon's hand and looked up at him. "You've come to a nice hospital with nice people. I hope you'll be as happy here as we were. And I've heard that Sister Murphy is beginning to think she might approve of you one day!"

Tom came over. "Another drink, anyone?"

Before they had time to refuse, Mary Wilson called that food was ready and led them through the cavernous hall to an equally cavernous dining room. Sally and Frances made a giggly visit to the rubber plant on the way.

CHAPTER FOURTEEN

St Paul's had just celebrated its bicentenary. It would have been impossible to guess that it had been built originally in fields well away from the town, a fever ward for patients with infectious diseases. Town and hospital had expanded over the centuries, and St Paul's was now a district hospital of five hundred beds in the suburbs of Market Houghton.

The architecture of the hospital reflected its spasmodic growth. Portacabins huddled in the shelter of a large Victorian building, now mainly offices. A modern postgraduate centre, glass and bright render, sat oddly beside the old fever ward, now pathology laboratories and the mortuary. Seen from the air, the new ward block was shaped like a cross with three wards in each of the four limbs. Upper South, Sister Murphy's, was the top ward in the south limb with Middle and Lower South below. Her friend Eileen Kenny had Lower East, acute surgical.

Simon arrived for his Monday round at exactly nine o'clock. Ward rounds on Upper South always began exactly on time. Two junior doctors were on his team: a houseman, newly qualified, and a registrar with three years more experience. Both, nervous of Sister Murphy, were already waiting. Simon was one of three physicians, and every third day and weekend, emergency admissions were his responsibility. His team had been on duty for the weekend and there were a number of new patients to be sorted. The round moved slowly from bed to bed, down one side of the ward and back up the other; the direction never varied. Simon's patients were all tucked up, clean and silent. Talking was forbidden during a consultant's round, and nurses and ward auxiliaries communicated in whispers. He reflected on the contrast between Upper South and his other ward, run by a progressive male charge nurse, where patients were referred to as clients and addressed by their Christian names, be they eighteen or eighty, and where the consultant was seen as an equal member of the "caring team". At least here he could concentrate on the diagnosis and expect to hear something down his stethoscope other than the ward cleaner's vacuum.

They were interrupted by the late arrival of Matthew Healey, a medical student on a three-month attachment to the hospital. Simon's registrar and houseman observed Matthew's dishevelled appearance with concern. He had obviously got out of bed in a hurry, but whose bed? Michael Randall, the registrar, had just started a two-year job rotation to St Paul's and already had a steady girlfriend in the nurses' home. The houseman, recently qualified and on his first appointment, had his eye on Daisy Thorpe, a pretty student nurse.

Most of the admissions on the round were routine. Over the weekend, Simon had accumulated the usual mix of heart attacks, strokes, pneumonias and overdoses. These had been dealt with effectively by the resident junior doctors, sometimes after phone calls for advice, and he needed only to ensure that nothing had been overlooked.

Eventually he came to a problem. A local farmer had been admitted on Saturday at the request of his GP, Tom Easter, whom Simon had met at Angus Wilson's a few days before. Embarrassed, and at his wife's insistence, he had consulted Tom because of unaccustomed weariness. Tom had immediately noticed his pallor. He was obviously anaemic, but there was more than that. The translucent, bone china appearance of his skin suggested an underlying infection, and when the nurse took his temperature it was slightly raised. Tom had known Mr Raspberry for years and could see that he was unwell. He immediately arranged his admission to St Paul's.

Simon looked at the temperature chart. There was a low-grade fever. Usually there would be an infection somewhere to account for this but it hadn't been found. Chest and urine were the usual suspects, but X-ray and water tests were normal. Blood samples were being cultured in the laboratory to see if they contained bacteria which might have been responsible, but it was still too early for a result.

Simon introduced himself and began to examine Mr Raspberry, beginning with his hands. He noticed at once the splinter haemorrhages under the fingernails. These tiny dark lines, exactly like splinters of wood, were common in people who worked with their hands, but sometimes they were more significant. He felt Mr Raspberry's pulse at the wrist, noting a tapping quality to the heartbeat. A glance at the blood pressure chart confirmed his suspicion and then, pleased at the opportunity of impressing his juniors and perhaps even Sister Murphy, he put his stethoscope in his ears and placed the bell over Mr Raspberry's heart, listening for the murmur of an incompetent aortic valve.

Normally the flow of blood through the heart is so smooth that it is virtually inaudible. Heart valves keep blood pumped silently in the right direction, but when they are damaged, perhaps by rheumatic fever in childhood, the stream becomes turbulent around them and murmurs are created. Medical students spend long hours puzzling over the different types of murmur which, according to quality and timing, indicate whether the damaged valve is obstructing forward flow or allowing blood to leak backwards.

Simon sat Mr Raspberry up, leant him forward and listened just to the right of his breastbone. He could hear a faint blowing sound. The function of the aortic valve is to stop backflow of blood which has already left the heart, and this murmur confirmed that it was leaking.

Matthew Healey watched all this with increasing concern. It looked as though Mr Raspberry was turning out to be a "good teaching case", and any moment now Dr Spence was likely to ask him to have a listen and, worse still, make a diagnosis. He slid behind the registrar, trying to be inconspicuous. "What's he found?"

"Where were you last night?"

"Daisy Thorpe."

The registrar relaxed. "Try aortic incompetence due to subacute bacterial endocarditis. Ask him if he's had any dental treatment lately."

Matthew moved out into view again. Simon told him to listen to Mr Raspberry's heart and was taken aback when he got the diagnosis right.

"Anything you'd like to ask him?"

"Have you seen a dentist recently?"

Now it was Mr Raspberry's turn to be impressed. "How could you possibly know that?" he asked.

***

After the ward round, drinking coffee in Sister Murphy's office, they discussed Mr Raspberry's treatment. A diagnosis of subacute bacterial endocarditis meant that his aortic valve had become infected with bacteria, which were eating away at it, making it leak. Dental work releases showers of bacteria into the bloodstream from their homes in the crevices amongst the teeth. Normally an army of white blood cells deals with these invaders instantly, but sometimes they find a place to hide. Heart valves are perfect hiding places, but the bacteria can't usually get a foothold on them as they sweep past in the stream of blood. However if the valve has been damaged and roughened, perhaps by childhood rheumatic fever as in Mr Raspberry's case, the smooth flow is disturbed and they can get a grip. Once established, a colony rapidly forms, growing all the time, steadily destroying the valve. Bits break off and get carried around the body in the blood, causing the splinter haemorrhages Simon had seen under his fingernails. The sudden fall in blood pressure when the heart relaxes in diastole and blood leaks back through through the damaged valve results in the tapping quality to the pulse that Simon had noticed. Persistent infection leads to increasing weakness, and if it is not treated in time, the valve gives way completely and the patient dies suddenly.

While they were talking, Simon's houseman phoned the bacteriologist, who confirmed that bacteria had been cultured from the blood sample.

"What's it likely to be?"

"Streptococcus viridans," Matthew said, now firmly in the registrar's debt.

"And the treatment?"

"Penicillin."

"Good," Simon said. "The bad news for Mr Raspberry is that it will take six weeks to clear the infection and he'll have to stay in hospital so we can give the penicillin into a vein. But we've got it in time, so he should be all right."

"Not always."

Simon looked at Sister Murphy in surprise. "Strep viridans is sensitive to penicillin."

"The last one wasn't." she said. "He was no better after three weeks and Dr Greenhalgh was beginning to get concerned. He was listening to his heart on the ward round when the valve gave way and he died in front of us."

"He would have had pulmonary oedema," Simon explained to Matthew. "When the valve gave way, back pressure in the blood vessels in his lungs would have poured fluid into the air spaces, drowning him."

"It came frothing out of his mouth and nose" Sister Murphy said. "Dr Greenhalgh stood still for several seconds, as though he couldn't believe what was happening, then he tried desperately to resuscitate the poor man. He even gave mouth to mouth before the crash team arrived. It was hopeless, of course."

"When was this?" Simon asked.

"Only last year. He walked off the ward as though he was sleep-walking. I never saw him alive again."

Simon looked away, embarrassed to see tears in her eyes.

CHAPTER FIFTEEN

After his ward round, Simon walked with Matthew Healey through the covered way to the old fever block which now housed Pathology. Matthew was a student at St Peter's Medical School in London. In their final year, students were expected to arrange a three-month attachment to another hospital to allow them to experience medicine elsewhere. His father had been friendly with Geoffrey Ayling at university and they had kept in touch. Geoffrey had approached Simon, who'd agreed to take Mathew under his wing. He was a good-looking lad, medium height, with fair hair, abundant freckles and brown eyes, a combination which had already caused a stir in the nurses' home.

The laboratories were at the front of the building, and Anthony Cosgrove, the bacteriologist, was waiting for them.

"There's no doubt," he said. "We've grown Strep viridans from every bottle." He showed them the petri dishes containing blood agar on which the bacterium was growing.

When the houseman had taken blood samples from Mr Raspberry, he had injected them at once into bottles containing a broth in which bacteria could survive and rapidly reproduce. These had been taken to the laboratory and incubated overnight. Next morning, the clear broth was cloudy, obviously containing organisms, which under the microscope looked like streptococci, but there are several members of this family of bacteria and it was important to determine which particular streptococcus this was and which antibiotic would kill it. A drop of broth was therefore smeared across the surface of the agar in flat round, plastic Petrie dishes. Agar is a firm jelly made from seaweed and bacteria thrive on it, forming colonies large enough to be seen by the naked eye and often distinctive enough to be identified. Different substances can be mixed in to encourage the growth of one type or inhibit another. Mr Raspberry's streptococcus was growing happily on agar mixed with horse's blood.

"The green colour tells us it's Streptococcus viridans," Doctor Cosgrove explained to Matthew. "The bacteria make a chemical which breaks down the blood and that's what produces the colour."

Matthew stared at the tiny round colonies, pale green against the red of the agar. "And because it's Strep viridans you know it will be sensitive to penicillin?"

"Yes, but we always check. Bacteria evolve and increasingly are becoming antibiotic resistant." He showed them another petri dish with a disc of blotting paper the size of a penny in one corner. Although the surface of the agar was covered in green colonies, none was growing within an inch of the paper which had been soaked in penicillin.

"Even though it's obviously sensitive, we won't treat Mr Raspberry with penicillin alone," Simon said to Matthew. "With endocarditis we always use a second antibiotic, gentamicin, to reinforce it. Bacteria on a heart valve are very difficult to get at, so we hit them as hard as we can. That's why we give very high doses straight into a vein rather than relying on tablets, and why we treat for six weeks. And even then it doesn't always work. A quarter of patients still die. Before antibiotics, of course, it was always fatal."

"So Dr Greenhalgh's patient was one of the quarter?" Matthew said.

"Dr Cosgrove looked at him in surprise. "Jimmy Greenhalgh's patient?"

"Sister Murphy told us about it," Simon explained. "Apparently he blew his valve on the ward round."

"Yes, I remember now. Jimmy was down here several times, worried that he wasn't responding to treatment. If you're really interested I'll ask my secretary to find the records."

"I can't understand why they don't get better if you use the right antibiotic," Matthew said to Simon while they waited.

"Maybe the diagnosis isn't made in time, or perhaps they're already weakened by another condition. You have to be pretty tough to withstand a heart infection like endocarditis."

Eventually Dr Cosgrove returned with a folder. "David Vass. Sixty-three years old. No past illnesses apart from rheumatic fever when he was a child, which must have damaged his valve but not enough ever to be a problem. Hadn't been ill for too long before his GP suspected the diagnosis and sent him up."

"So really he should have been cured by the antibiotics." Simon took the records and searched for Mr Vass' temperature charts. Endocarditis causes a mild fever which usually settles within ten days of starting treatment, a good indication that the antibiotics are going to work.

"It doesn't look as though he responded at all," he said, showing the charts to Matthew. "No wonder Dr Greenhalgh was getting worried."

"Can you measure antibiotic levels in his blood to see if he's getting enough?" Matthew asked.

"We always measure gentamicin levels because it's a dangerous drug if you give too much. We don't bother with penicillin because it's safe even in the very high doses we use in endocarditis." Simon thumbed through the notes. "Mr Vass' gentamicin levels were fine."

He was surprised and pleased at Matthew's interest and keen to foster it.

"We'll go over to histopathology. Mr Vass probably had a post-mortem, and maybe we can find out what his valve actually looked like."

They thanked Anthony Cosgrove and walked the short distance to Angus Wilson's empire at the back of the old fever block.

"I remember Mr Vass very well," Angus told them. "Usually when an aortic valve gives way the patient survives long enough to be transferred to a cardiac centre so a heart surgeon can have a go at repairing it, although if the infection is still there it's almost doomed to failure. So it's an unusual case for me. Actually, I can do better that tell you what I found, I can show it to you."

He led them through to the pathology museum. Here Angus preserved for ever in glass jars of formalin the most interesting bits of his most interesting patients. Matthew stared, fascinated, at colons, bladders, lungs and brains, tidily arranged and labelled on shelves which stretched from the floor to the low ceiling. They found Mr Vass' aortic valve at the end of a row, nestled between an eye and a testicle, and Angus pointed out how one cusp had been eaten away by the infection.

The aortic valve has three leafs, or cusps, which fold smoothly upwards when blood is ejected through them by contraction of the heart, and fall back to fit perfectly together when the heart relaxes and fills again. One of them was deformed by a knobbly vegetation and had partially torn from its attachment.

"That's what happened on the ward round," Angus said. "It ruptured. That's what killed him."

"Did you get a culture from the valve?" Simon asked.

"Yes. And it was a pure growth of Strep viridans, completely sensitive to penicillin."

"Which never touched it,' Simon said. "How odd."

Matthew left for a tutorial and Angus offered Simon a coffee. They sat in his pleasant, light office with a view of the silver birch wood at the back of the fever block. There was a large microscope and a pile of slides beside the window. Angus' work was divided between post-mortem examinations and microscopic examination of the lumps, bumps and organs removed with varying degrees of necessity by the hospital surgeons. This morning, he had been working in the mortuary, and Simon was aware of the smell of formalin and death which still clung to his clothes.

"Settling in all right?" Angus asked.

A consultant's post was the most important achievement of a hospital doctor's career and usually the greatest upheaval for the family—a move, often for life, to an unfamiliar part of the world away from relatives and friends. Angus had seen many new arrivals in his twenty-five years at St Paul's; some made good colleagues and some not so good, but his first instincts about them were usually correct, and he was happy with Simon.

While Simon chatted, Angus thought about his old friend. Jimmy had come to St Paul's a few years after himself. Then, it was a small undeveloped district hospital with fifteen consultants. Now there were fifty, reflecting the expansion of peripheral hospitals over the last two decades at the expense of larger centres. Angus and his colleagues had seen this coming and wanted to attract the brighter young doctors who themselves were nervous of leaving the teaching hospitals.

Jimmy had made a brief visit to St Paul's after the post was advertised, and Angus had liked him at once. He invited him back two weeks later, and the Greenhalghs had stayed at the Old Rectory. Each family had a girl and boy of roughly the same age and it was a successful weekend. It was summer and Angela was impressed by the house and its large garden. Jimmy had liked everything about Norfolk—the long sandy beaches, the feeling of peaceful space, the endless sky—but worried that he was opting out of the possibility of an academic career.

Angus had invited Tom and Caroline Easter over for Sunday lunch. All three couples got on well. They were roughly the same age, and the Easter children, boy and girl again, played happily with the other four.

Now, talking to Simon, he was reminded again how much he missed his friend. He thought of the contrast between Jimmy and his successor. Both were tall men but Simon was fair and thin while Jimmy was darker and heavier. Simon was intense and at times could seem uptight and humourless. Jimmy, on the other hand, was instantly relaxing. He used his bulk to reassure patients rather than intimidate them, and they succumbed quickly to his easy charm. He was an instinctive doctor, aware that medicine was as much black magic as science, knowing that the performance was often more important than the pills.

The couples had become close friends. The Greenhalghs bought an old doctor's house in a village a few miles from Market Houghton and renovated it slowly over the years. The Easters lived nearby and the three families grew up together, their children as likely to be in one house at the weekend as another.

St Paul's expanded as more physicians and surgeons were appointed. Within a few years most of the original consultants had retired, leaving Jimmy and Angus, in their mid-forties, amongst the most senior in the hospital.

Simon thanked him for the coffee, and Angus thought again of the circumstances of his friend's death. He had apparently gone straight to his office after the ward round when Mr Vass had died. According to his secretary, he had stayed there on his own until lunchtime and then left without a word. Nobody remembered seeing him after that. He hadn't turned up for his afternoon clinic, something that had never happened before, and his registrar had covered for him. The next day, Angela phoned Angus. Jimmy still hadn't come home and there'd been no message from him. That morning, unknown to them, the birdwatcher had found his body.

CHAPTER SIXTEEN

Sally Spence waited for Harry outside the windswept primary school. Several other mothers also waited, chatting in small groups or sitting together in cars. Occasionally they acknowledged Sally, but she hadn't made any friends amongst them. Society here was insular and self-sufficient, politely disinterested in newcomers, and she was increasingly lonely.

Harry ran out and hugged her. He was alone as usual, withdrawn and subdued, quite unlike the gregarious little boy they had bought from London. Of course it was early days, and a major move like this was bound to be difficult for all of them, but it would have helped, she thought, if Simon had been around more often. He left early and came home long after his son's bedtime.

Harry wouldn't discuss his day and Sally knew he wasn't happy. He had been a bright, intelligent child but now he had lost his sparkle. He cheered up slightly as they left the school behind and approached their new house, but Sally didn't. She couldn't get used to its bland symmetry, its artexed ceilings, and the small garden was completely exposed. All in all, she was thoroughly fed up, and if it hadn't been for Frances Swynnerton, she thought uneasily, she might have gone back to London long ago.

They had become friends after the dinner party at Angus Wilson's. Frances was widowed and childless and she was lonely too. She was a few years older than Sally but they shared a sense of humour and were easy in each other's company. She started work early and was sometimes home by mid-afternoon, when she would phone Sally and invite her to bring Harry over to the coast for tea and a walk on Massingham Beach. The phone was ringing today as Sally opened the front door and, happier now, they gathered together Harry's bucket, spades and kite and got back in the car.

"Beach first, tea later," Frances said to Harry when they arrived.

Behind her cottage, a path led straight to the marshes and, beyond them, to Massingham Beach. The sea lavender was in flower, and Harry picked a bunch for Frances as they walked to the sand dunes. The cloudless Norfolk sky stretched for ever and the breeze was cool and salty fresh.

After several kamikaze flights of his kite, Harry noticed the wreck. It was low tide, a big spring tide, and the sea was several hundred yards away. The ship was dry, chunks of its superstructure sticking high above the sand. Frances was reluctant when Sally suggested walking out to it but eventually agreed, and they set out across the vast beach. Frances told Harry the story of the *Jura*, from its bunkering days to its Massingham grave, and he made a song about it and chanted as they walked.

After fifteen minutes they were there. Harry touched the cold, rusty, corroded metal and shivered. There were deep pools around in the sand, and mussels and seaweed clung to the bits of superstructure and railing that remained. He held tight to Sally's hand as they explored it, fascinated and frightened. She inhaled the dank air and turned suddenly to Frances.

"Is this where Dr Greenhalgh died?"

Frances glanced at Harry. "Yes," she said, "but we've got to go."

The tide had arrived, creeping across the sand and flooding into the pools. They started for the shore, dragging Harry between them, splashing through streams and rivulets. After twenty minutes, well ahead of the sea, they turned and stared at the wreck. Already the railings had vanished and only the superstructure remained.

Over tea Sally asked about Simon's predecessor's death, but Frances could add little to what she already knew. It appeared to be a particularly nasty murder but the police had no leads. Frances seemed subdued and Sally didn't press her. Tea wasn't much fun, and the long walk had tired Harry. They left earlier than usual for the sterile comforts of their artexed home.

CHAPTER SEVENTEEN

When Matthew Healey's bleep went off at midnight he was in bed with Daisy Thorpe.

"Don't answer it," she whispered in his ear.

Matthew didn't see how he could answer it. He could hardly phone the hospital switchboard from the nurses' home in the middle of the night. They started again where they had left off.

Dr Spence's registrar and houseman were in the casualty department.

"Bleep him every five minutes until he answers," the registrar said.

After the third bleep, Matthew sighed, kissed Daisy, got out of bed, dressed silently and tiptoed down the stairs to the basement and the open window behind the swimming pool. When he got back to his room in the doctors' residence, he picked up the phone.

"Matthew, where the hell have you been?"

"Sorry. I was so deeply asleep I didn't hear the first ones."

"So how do you know you'd been bleeped? Come down to casualty, quick as you can."

Matthew found Michael Randall, the registrar, in the resuscitation room, where the sickest patients received emergency treatment.

"Ever seen a case of meningitis?" Michael asked.

Matthew hadn't. She was a girl in her late teens, obviously very ill, hardly responding to questions.

"She got like this so quickly," her frightened mother said. "She went to bed early saying she'd felt fluey during the day and had a nasty headache. It was so unusual for Polly to do this that I looked in on her before I went to bed, and I could hardly wake her up." She began to cry. "She didn't seem to recognise me."

A staff nurse put her arm around her and took her out of the cubicle.

Polly had a high temperature. Michael put his hand under her head and tried to flex her neck, but it was so stiff he could lift her shoulders off the bed. He raised the sheet and showed Matthew the spots on her legs and tummy.

"There are already more of these than when she arrived half an hour ago. She's very sick. The stiff neck and temperature mean she's got meningitis, and the spots mean it's caused by the meningococcus bacterium, the most dangerous type. Luckily her GP made the diagnosis when her mother called him and gave her a shot of penicillin while waiting for the ambulance. Literally minutes count in giving the antibiotic when they're as sick as this."

"Is that what's in the drip?"

"Yes. We'll flood her with penicillin now and just hope we've got it in time."

The nurse had come back with a trolley, and they rolled Polly on her side for the lumbar puncture with difficulty, as she was confused and struggled. Matthew helped restrain her while the registrar injected local anaesthetic and then deftly slipped a long, thin spinal needle deep into her lower back between the lumbar vertebrae.

Cerebrospinal fluid bathes the brain and spinal cord. It is normally crystal clear, but Polly's was cloudy as it dripped from the needle into a bottle, confirming the diagnosis.

Her blood pressure was falling and they decided to move her to the intensive care unit. Because she was so ill, Michael phoned Dr Spence at home. He agreed with the diagnosis and treatment.

"She's developing septic shock," he said. "She may die whatever you do. If she survives the night she'll have a chance. Let me know if she deteriorates."

Polly was rushed to intensive care, where an X-ray confirmed that the infection was beginning to damage her lungs. She was heavily sedated and a tube inserted into her windpipe so a ventilator could breathe for her. By now her blood pressure was dangerously low and drugs were given to increase it and protect her kidneys, which were beginning to fail. She was given steroids to counter the shock.

"That's all we can do," Michael said.

A nurse told them that Polly's father had arrived, and they went together to talk to him. They found her parents stunned.

"How can it happen so quickly to a healthy girl?" her father asked.

Matthew listened as Michael explained Polly's illness to them. They were worried it would spread to her brother and sister, and he reassured them that although this hardly ever happened, they would give the family an antibiotic to protect them.

"Please do all you can," Polly's father said.

Matthew's eyes pricked with tears, and he turned away to hide them. Polly was only a few years younger than him.

The registrar left to get some sleep, and Matthew stayed with Polly in intensive care. By dawn, there were signs that she was beginning to improve, and by nine o'clock, when Dr Spence arrived, her blood pressure had stabilised and her temperature was falling.

"I think she'll be one of the lucky ones," he said.

He checked the dose of penicillin—four million units, which was more than adequate. He was cautiously optimistic with her parents. Sister Finoula Murphy from the medical ward had sat through the night with them. She was a close friend of Polly's mother and had known Polly for most of her life. If all went well, he told them, she might be off the ventilator within twenty-four hours.

Matthew was tired but elated that Polly was improving. Dr Spence excused him for the rest of the morning, and he went back to his own bed for a few hours' sleep.

He woke at midday, showered and shaved, and came straight down to the unit. It was obvious at once that something was wrong. There was a huddle of doctors at Polly's bed. The improvement hadn't lasted. By mid-morning her blood pressure had fallen again, and the blotchy rash was spreading rapidly. Now the meningococcus was winning the battle for Polly's life. She was increasingly dependent on the drugs to maintain her circulation, and her kidneys had stopped working. Her lungs were so damaged that the ventilator was struggling to provide her with oxygen.

Polly died at four thirty that afternoon. Dr Spence left to tell her parents, returning white-faced, and Matthew heard her mother sobbing as he walked away from intensive care.

CHAPTER EIGHTEEN

They were all upset by Polly's death, but Matthew was particularly affected.

"She seemed to be getting better when I left in the morning," he said. "The penicillin must have been working. So what happened?"

Dr Spence had no answer, but he knew how unpredictable and dangerous the meningococcus was. Most of the time it lived a blameless existence in the mouths of perhaps a third of the population. Very rarely, and for no obvious reason, it would invade the bloodstream and change from a harmless passenger to a vicious killer. It particularly liked to infect the meninges, the lining of the brain and spinal cord, causing meningitis. This was bad enough, but the real danger occurred when rampant bacteria were spread around the body by the bloodstream. It was this condition, septicaemia, which had killed Polly.

"We get cases most years," he said, "usually young people, and I'm afraid we expect to lose some whatever we do."

To distract Matthew, he told him to gather the last few cases of meningococcal infection from the hospital diagnostic index and study them. Perhaps if he understood the condition better, he would find it easier to come to terms with Polly's death.

When patients are discharged from hospital or die, their diagnosis is stored on computer. The next morning, Matthew asked the staff in the medical records department for the names of all patients with meningococcal infection admitted in the last two years. There

were seven including Polly. Patient confidentiality was strictly protected at St Paul's, so his consultant had signed an authorisation for
Matthew to obtain the notes. The hospital folders were logged out
to him, and he took them to the library in the Postgraduate Centre.

He had been asked to look specifically at whether the general
practitioner had injected penicillin at home, whether there were
signs of the dreaded septicaemia and, of course, the outcome, survival or death. This was harder than he had expected. The notes
were bulky and haphazardly filed. It took the rest of the morning
just to achieve some sort of order and extract the information he
wanted. After a hurried lunch in the hospital canteen, he returned
to the library to collect the folders, already late for the afternoon
ward round. He ran up the stairs, dumped the notes on Sister Murphy's desk, and rushed onto the ward, grinning at Daisy Thorpe,
who passed him with a brimming bedpan.

When the consultant's round was over, they settled in the office.
Sister Murphy made coffee and Matthew told them what he had
found.

"Other than Polly, there have been six cases in the last two years.
They were all admitted within three weeks in March last year."

"It's not too unusual to have a cluster like that," Dr Spence said,
"especially in the winter months, although you don't usually find
any contact between them. Perhaps the colds and flu around at that
time weakens their immunity sufficiently for the bacteria to move
in. Did any of them die?"

"All the cases in the cluster died."

"Surely not all of them."

"No, he's right," Sister Murphy said. "Four of them died on this
ward."

Dr Spence took the notes and quickly scanned them. "There's
only five folders here."

"I must have left one in the library." Matthew was embarrassed.
"I was sure I picked them all up."

Dr Spence was very annoyed. "You can't leave confidential information lying around for anyone to read," he snapped. "Go back down now and get them."

Matthew left the office, scarlet with humiliation. The folder was lying on his desk in the library. He brought it back and endured another lecture before the notes were opened.

"This is one of the March patients," Dr Spence said after a while, "but I think some pages are missing. A day seems to be lost from the doctor's records."

Matthew hadn't noticed but he wasn't surprised. He explained how the notes had been hopelessly jumbled and it had taken him most of the morning just to get them into some sort of order. Ward clerks, who filed the notes, were overworked and badly paid and it had always been difficult to recruit enough of them.

He started again. "As I said, there were six cases in March last year. They all died. The first two didn't get penicillin at home but the other four did."

"That tends to happen. Meningococcal infection is rare and looks very much like flu at the start. It's almost impossible to diagnose early, and it's only when GPs hear there are cases around that they start to look specifically for it. Polly's doctor recognised it because of the neck stiffness and rash, but it's not always that easy."

"It didn't save her, being treated early, and it didn't help the other four either."

"Were they all very ill when they came in?"

"I don't think so. Only two of them had the rash and other signs of septicaemia, and they went straight to intensive care. The other four were admitted here."

Dr Spence looked at Sister Murphy, who was staring down the ward through the office window. She had been very subdued over the last few days. He remembered she had been with Polly's family in intensive care when he broke the news of her death. She had excused herself today from the second half of the ward round, handing over to a senior staff nurse.

"Do you recall them, sister?" he said gently.

"I remember them well; by the time they arrived here, the signs of meningitis were obvious but they weren't terribly ill. They were conscious and lucid and on penicillin drips, which had been started immediately in casualty. Dr Greenhalgh was sure they'd be all right."

"But they weren't?"

"No. They just didn't improve; they got steadily worse. They were all dead within forty-eight hours of admission."

Dr Spence had to leave then for a meeting, but before he went, he watched Matthew gather all six folders together to return them to medical records.

***

Later that evening, comfortably entwined with Daisy in her warm bed, Matthew relived his embarrassment. "I felt such a fool! I know I was rushing, but I was sure I collected all the notes from the library after lunch. I realise now that it was stupid to leave them there."

"I saw the notes in Sister Murphy's office," Daisy said. "I came in for something and she was looking through them. I was surprised she wasn't on the consultant's round. She asked me why the notes weren't filed in the ward trolley. Then she realised they didn't belong to patients on the ward. She was cross and told me to go away and leave her alone. She's not usually like that. I had to come back to the office later, but she wasn't there."

"And the notes?"

"They were piled tidily on her desk."

"Remember what we did last time?" Matthew said.

Daisy did.

CHAPTER NINETEEN

The day after Matthew's humiliation with the notes, he had gone to Massingham Beach for a walk with Daisy Thorpe. He collected her from the nurses' home in the afternoon in his battered Austin Healey Sprite. The passenger door was jammed, as usual, and he watched her with interest as she wriggled across from the driver's seat in her tight jeans.

"There's lots of dunes," he said hopefully, but Daisy was non-committal, knowing how uncomfortable sand in the wrong places could be.

They found a row of deserted beach huts on the edge of the golf course looking out over the sea. Several had been broken into and vandalised, but eventually they discovered one that was open and reasonably clean. Best of all was a single iron bed with a tatty mattress...

Later, as they walked on the beach, he talked about the hospital notes. "There's something odd about it, Daisy. I was stupid to leave all the notes on the library desk during lunch where anybody could read them, but I can't understand why I only collected five sets and left one behind."

"You were rushing! You charged past me when you came onto the ward."

"I suppose so. But I'd left the notes in a pile on top of each other. Why would I take the top five and leave one behind?"

"I don't know, but you did. When Dr Spence sent you back down to the library, you said they were still on the desk."

"Unless somebody had borrowed them during lunch and put them back later, after I'd collected the others."

Daisy stared at him. "Why would anybody do that?"

He was silent, and they walked along the beach for a time, scrunching the shells beneath their feet.

"Let's go and look at that boat," Matthew said.

The tide was out, and a few hundred yards towards the sea, a houseboat leaned at an uncomfortable angle on the hard sand.

"Hallo. Lovely day!" A white haired man in his seventies had appeared on deck, looking down at them over half-moon spectacles.

"How did you run aground?" Matthew asked.

"All Fay's fault. She bought me a cup of tea at a crucial moment when we were leaving Massingham Harbour and I lost my concentration."

"It's always my fault," Mrs Housen said cheerfully, coming to the rail beside him.

"Aren't you worried about the waves when the tide comes in?"

Mr Housen looked out to the distant sea. "It looks calm enough. Anyhow, the coastguard around here are very helpful. Perhaps I'll call them up and ask them to stand by. That wreck makes me nervous. The tide always seems to pull you towards it."

Matthew and Daisy noticed the *Jura* for the first time, its black superstructure shimmering in the hot sunlight several hundred yards away.

"Come up, if you'd like, and have a cup of tea." Mr Housen lowered a solid wooden ladder and they climbed the ten feet to *Altimeter*'s deck. Matthew could see now that it wasn't an ordinary houseboat.

"It's an old lifeboat hull," Mr Housen explained. "The last owner bought it for a song and turned it into his home. He lived on it in Boston Harbour for years and never went to sea."

"And then we bought it," Fay chipped in. "Best thing we ever did. We sold our house and now we're water gypsies, wandering the harbours and havens of the Wash. I just wish we'd had some work done on the engine."

"There's nothing wrong with the engine," her husband said. "These old diesels go on for ever."

"Ours doesn't, dear. It keeps stopping and refusing to start again, usually when we least want it to."

"Come and look inside," Mr Housen said, changing the subject.

The previous owner had made *Altimeter* into a compact, cosy home. They climbed down the companionway into a light saloon with comfortable seats and a well-equipped galley. Matthew had done some sailing himself and looked without success for the usual navigation aids and chart table.

"How do you find your way around?" he asked.

"Oh, I think we know the Wash pretty well," Mr Housen said vaguely, "and there's always the radio if we get lost."

Matthew grinned, making a mental note never to go to sea in *Altimeter*. They sat around the saloon table holding mugs of tea. The boat wasn't designed to sit on the sand and leant uncomfortably, but the Housens were used to it.

Fay asked if they were on holiday. Daisy explained that she was a student nurse at St Paul's.

"Isn't that where poor Jimmy Greenhalgh worked?"

"That's right. He was a physician there. He died last year." She looked at Matthew. "Dr Spence is his successor."

Mr Housen glanced at his wife. "Do you know how he died?"

"Of course; he was murdered. We talked about nothing else for months. His body was found handcuffed to the wreck, just over there."

Matthew went up on deck and stared at the wreck. "Who did it?"

"Nobody knows."

Matthew and Daisy waited on the sand dunes till the tide came in and saw *Altimeter* float off uneventfully under the watchful eye of the Wells inshore lifeboat. He was thoughtful as they drove back to the hospital.

"All those meningitis deaths were Dr Greenhalgh's patients, weren't they? Not a good year for him, one way and another."

***

The next day, Matthew went down to the medical records department. He still had the chit from Dr Spence authorising him to withdraw the notes. He had returned all six sets after the ward round two days before, and now he asked only for the file of the painter, the last patient to die. These were the notes he was supposed to have left in the library, and he remembered Dr Spence discovering that pages were missing from them. The records clerk was gone for several minutes.

"They're not here," she said. "They've been signed out again."

Matthew thought for a moment. "Can you tell me who's got them, please?"

The clerk sighed; she was middle-aged, overworked and impervious to Matthew's charms. She checked on the computer. Matthew looked over her shoulder as she typed on the keyboard.

"They've gone to Upper South ward."

"Who requested them?"

She typed again; Sister Murphy's name appeared on the screen.

CHAPTER TWENTY

Harry clung to Sally so tightly when she kissed him goodnight that she had to prise his arms from around her neck. "We're going to Frances' cottage. Shall I give her a kiss from you?"

He smiled and snuggled into bed. "A big one."

"Do you know who's going to be there?" Simon asked on the drive over, swerving suddenly to avoid a suicidal pheasant.

Sally grabbed dramatically for the door handle. "It's safer to run over them."

"I know," he said irritably, "but why kill them if you can avoid it."

"Better a pheasant than us. Think of Harry."

Simon stamped on the brakes. "For Christ's sake." He glared at her, gripping the steering wheel. "Don't be so bloody sanctimonious."

She was shocked by his anger, and they sat for a few minutes in silence in the middle of the country lane, breathing deeply.

Simon spoke first. "All right, I'm sorry!"

"I should hope so! Just as well I was wearing my seat belt."

"I knew you were wearing it."

She said nothing, and they drove on. After a while he looked across.

"I'm sorry."

Sally smiled reluctantly. "Me too."

"I suppose I just don't want to socialise," he said. "It's been a long day."

"But you like Frances."

He didn't reply, and eventually they came to the cottage in Massingham Staithe.

Frances kissed them both in the tiny hallway, squeezing Simon's hand for a few seconds before he followed Sally through to the sitting room. The Easters were there already. Caroline chatted to Sally while Frances fetched drinks, firmly refusing Tom's offer of help. Eventually, while the three women sat together on the sofa, deep in gossip, Tom and Simon went out through the back door into the small garden, where they stood looking out across the low flint wall to the marshes and the distant North Sea. It was the middle of July but the easterly wind made them shiver in their light jackets.

"Settled in?" Tom asked.

"Just about."

"It's easier for you than for Sally, I expect. It's a big upheaval."

"It's been difficult at times, but Frances has been very kind."

Tom looked at him curiously. The door from the sitting room to the hall had been open when the Spences arrived, and he'd thought that Frances had held on to Simon's hand longer than necessary. "Do you see much of her?"

"Sally does," Simon said quietly, "and she's very good with Harry."

Tom stared out across the North Sea, towards the wreck. He had wondered occasionally about the relationship between his dead friend and the hospital pharmacist. Perhaps she had a thing for consultant physicians.

"How's Mr Raspberry doing?" he asked.

Simon remembered that his endocarditis patient had been sent into hospital by Tom. He was relieved to get off the subject of Frances. "Not as well as he should. He started off fine. His temperature was down after just a few days of antibiotics, but it was back a week later and he still has a fever now, after three weeks of treatment."

"Do you think the penicillin isn't working?"

"There's no reason why it shouldn't. I asked the lab to recheck the sensitivity of the bacterium on the original samples, and penicillin is definitely effective against it. Sometimes the antibiotics themselves can produce a temperature when they're injected straight into a vein, so that might be the explanation. Anyway, our visiting cardiologist has had a look at him and doesn't think there's an immediate risk of the valve failing."

Frances joined them.

"We're talking about Mr Raspberry on Upper South," Simon said.

Tom grinned at her. "Are you sure your penicilin's OK? You're not buying Albanian stuff on the cheap?"

"Look who's talking! Everybody knows that dispensing GPs buy the cheapest drugs they can get."

Tom smiled. "Don't listen to her," he said to Simon.

Frances was a good cook. They had samphire and a Cromer crab salad. The Spences had never tasted the Norfolk seaweed before. Frances told them it had been collected on the marshes behind her cottage, and Tom explained how to suck the green flesh off the stalk.

They talked eventually about Jimmy Greenhalgh. It had only been eight months since his death.

"The worst thing for Angela is having no explanation," Caroline said. "The police have no idea who killed him."

"Or why." Frances looked at Tom. "Everybody liked him, didn't they?"

"I thought so, but it seems somebody didn't. Maybe it was a patient with a grudge. That happens, and you've no idea why they hate you. Just a single word, an inflection in your voice, an opinion they didn't want."

Sally shivered. "Not a reason for murder. And such a horrible death!"

"Didn't Jimmy have an endocarditis patient like Mr Raspberry?" Frances asked suddenly. "Somebody who wasn't getting better when they should have done."

"I heard about that," Simon said. "Anthony Cosgrove told me, and Angus showed me the post-mortem specimen. I think he died the day Jimmy went missing."

"Not one of mine," Tom said. "News to me."

The babysitter phoned during the summer pudding. Harry wouldn't settle. He was downstairs, crying all the time, and she sounded fed up.

"We'll have to go," Sally said wearily. "She's only fourteen."

The Easters stayed for half an hour after Simon and Sally had gone.

"He's a bit uptight," Tom said, "but he's a good doctor. He's very different to Jimmy. I must say I miss him a lot."

"We all do," his wife said.

Frances was silent.

CHAPTER TWENTY-ONE

"Why don't you go and ask her?" Daisy said. "She won't bite you."

They were discussing the missing notes.

"I know I took all the folders from the library that were on the desk," Matthew said yet again. "Somebody must have pinched a set during lunch and put them back after I'd taken the others to the ward."

"Why would anybody do that?" Daisy, by now, was bored with the whole subject.

"Because they wanted to remove something from them before it was seen by Dr Spence. When he looked through the notes after I'd gone back to the library to get them, he said that some pages were missing. I bet that's why the notes were taken."

"Is that why you tried to get them back from medical records? To see what was missing?"

"Yes, or to see if it had been put back. But now Sister Murphy's got them."

"Could she have taken the pages out? Do you remember how she left the ward round early and I found her in the office looking at the notes? She could have done it then."

"But I've told you that particular folder wasn't in her office – it was down in the library."

"Where you left it!"

"I *didn't* leave it there." Matthew was getting angry.

"Perhaps you don't want to believe you left it there. And don't get cross with me, Mathew Healey."

He relaxed. They were sitting on the edge of her bed in the nurses' home, and he leant across and kissed her. "I'm sorry. I just can't
get it out of my mind."

Daisy stroked his cheek. "Then I think you should go and talk
to Sister Murphy about it. She won't bite."

***

Finoula Murphy had a soft spot for Matthew. She had seen dozens
of medical students come and go over the years, and he was no lazi-
er or randier than most of them. She had noticed that he was always
kind to the ward patients and gentle when he examined them, and
she remembered how upset he had been at Polly's death.

She was sitting behind her desk, working on the ward rota,
when Matthew stuck his head around the office door and asked if
he could talk to her. She invited him in, noting with surprise that
he closed the door behind him.

"Well?"

"I'm sorry to bother you like this," he began nervously. "It's
about the notes."

"What notes?"

"The ones I collected for Dr Spence on the meningitis patients."

She stared at him impassively for several seconds, and he shifted
uneasily.

"If it's not convenient now I can come back."

"'Sit down, Matthew. What about the notes?"

Her office was a prefabricated addition immediately inside the
ward on the right-hand side. It wasn't large but there was room for a
desk, a few chairs and some filing cabinets. A filter coffee machine,
a gift from a grateful patient, stood on a small corner table. A large
window provided a full view of the length of the ward from the
chair behind her desk. The door into the office, shut by Matthew,
was immediately on the right after the ward entrance. Ventilation

was provided by a high window, permanently open above the bay for the drug trolley on the ward side of the door.

"I felt such a fool when Dr Spence thought I'd left a folder in the library."

"So you should have done. There's a lot of private information in hospital notes. How would you feel if somebody left a file with personal details about you lying around for anyone to read?"

"I know. That's not what I mean." He paused.

"Well, go on, what do you mean?"

"I don't think I left the notes in the library when I came up to the ward for the round. I think somebody took them while I was at lunch."

She stared at him. "Why would anybody do that, Matthew. And anyhow, the folder was there when Dr Spence sent you down to find it."

"They must have put it back again."

"Oh come on! Why are you bringing this nonsense to me? It sounds as though you don't want to accept responsibility for being stupid. Have you said this to anybody else?"

He decided not to mention Daisy. "I haven't talked to anybody about it."

He would probably have given up at this stage had he not seen a flicker of relief on Sister Murphy's face.

"I think the notes were taken from the library so some pages could be removed," he went on boldly. "Dr Spence said he thought some of the doctor's notes were missing."

She snorted. "That's not surprising with the state of the folders these days."

He took a deep breath. "And I think you also believe that some pages were removed."

"Me!" She stood up and leaned angrily across the desk towards him. "Now you want to involve me in this fantasy?"

"And I think that's why you removed the notes from medical records: to see if something has been taken out."

She subsided back into her chair. "How do you know I've got the notes?"

"I tried to get them myself."

She said nothing, and he went on, "You must think it's important to have gone to the trouble."

She stood up and moved to the coffee machine. "I'll make us a cup. Milk and sugar?"

She didn't speak again until the coffee was brewed, and Matthew waited, wondering anxiously if he had gone too far. She handed him a cup, put her own on the desk and then went to the office door and opened it. There was nobody around, but she noticed that the lid to the drug trolley had been left open; presumably one of her nurses had forgotten to lock it. Tut-tutting irritably, she fetched her own key, then came back into the office and closed the door firmly behind her.

"You're quite right, Matthew," she said when she was seated behind her desk again. "I've got the notes back into some sort of order, and a page at least is missing."

"Why is it so important?"

"Patients' records are legal documents. They should never be interfered with. If this poor man's relatives decided to sue the hospital for whatever reason, the lawyers would have a field day when they found parts of the notes were missing"

"Can you tell what was in the missing pages, or who would take them?"

"I've no idea."

"The relatives!" Matthew said excitedly. "The patient's relatives. Perhaps they *are* going to sue. Missing pages would look like a cover-up."

"That's a bit far-fetched. How would they know you'd taken the notes out of the records department?"

"Maybe they know somebody who works here. You can trace the whereabouts of notes from any terminal on the hospital computer system."

She thought for a while. "I suppose it's not such a daft idea. The local press made a lot of fuss about the meningitis cases at the time, trying to make out the hospital was at fault. People might think there was mileage in suing. Was there anybody in the library that morning you didn't recognise?"

He shook his head. "I don't think so."

"Can you remember who was there? Was Mrs Swynnerton there?

"The pharmacy lady?" Matthew was surprised. "Why her?"

"No reason really, but she's in the library a lot so she could have been there. And if she was, she might have noticed somebody else."

He nodded. "She *was* there. She came and talked to me just before I went to lunch."

"Can you remember what she said?"

"I can, actually. She asked what I was doing, and I told her Dr Spence wanted to see the meningitis notes and I was going through them."

"Was she still in the library when you went for lunch?"

"I think so. She hadn't been there long."

"Was anybody else in the library when you left?"

"I can't remember anybody. But you're not suggesting she took the notes?"

"Of course not."

"Will you tell Dr Spence I didn't leave the notes in the library?"

"I still don't know if you did or not. The pages could have been lost on the ward. The notes were in a right mess. But I've got to talk to him about it, and I'll say it may well not have been your fault," she said kindly.

"What do you think he'll do?"

"Not much he can do, really. He'll probably tell the medical records manager and try to frighten him into finding the money for another ward clerk. Managers are terrified of litigation."

"Thanks for listening to me." He looked at his watch and jumped up. "I've got to rush. I hadn't realised it was this late."

"Where are you off to now?

"Supper at the Aylings'. He's a local farmer,"

"Geoffrey Ayling?"

"That's right. He's an old school-friend of my dad's. He's the reason I'm here. I'd never heard of St Paul's until he told Dad about it. I think he's something to do with the place."

"He's on the hospital board," Finoula said grimly. "Remember me to him."

Matthew rushed off, nearly colliding with Frances Swynnerton in the short corridor leading to the lift.

"Never run in the hospital unless it's a real emergency," she said crossly.

Sister Murphy cleared away the coffee cups and followed Matthew onto the ward. The drug trolley was in its proper place under the high, open office window, but the lid had been left open again. Angrily, she fetched her key and locked it.

CHAPTER TWENTY-TWO

Geoffrey Ayling's father looked down from above the mantelpiece at his son's guests, who were drinking gin and tonic and waiting for Matthew.

"His dad was late for everything," Geoffrey said, smiling.

The phone rang and Fiona answered it.

"His car won't start," she told them, "but he's got a lift. We'll wait for him."

"Time for another drink."

He arrived twenty minutes later, and Fiona introduced him to the other guests. There were two girls of his own age, their daughter Helen and Jimmy Greenhalgh's daughter Liz. Jimmy's wife Angela made up the small party of six. Matthew had talked to Daisy a lot about Jimmy's death since meeting the Housens on their grounded boat, and seeing Angela and her daughter now for the first time, he wondered how they had survived the horror.

"I was telling them your father was late for everything at school," Geoffrey said to Matthew with a grin. "You've obviously inherited the tendency."

"I'm very sorry. I was talking to Sister Murphy and didn't notice the time, and then my car wouldn't start."

"Sister Murphy; I've heard that name before." Fiona thought for a moment. "Isn't she the one who came round here that evening?"

"That's her," Geoffrey said.

"She asked to be remembered to you," Matthew said.

"Did she indeed?"

She hadn't been particularly pleased with him the last time they met, he thought. He'd seen her again after talking to Jimmy about the syringes. He'd checked with stores, and she was quite right; Upper South had used no more syringes in March than in other months.

"It doesn't fit in with the sterile water, I quite agree," he'd said to her. "I've talked to Dr Greenhalgh about it, and he thinks it's odd as well, but we can't see that it gets us anywhere. Anyhow, we're grateful to you for pointing it out."

"What were you talking about?" he asked now.

Matthew explained about the notes. Geoffrey was interested and listened carefully.

"Do you really think they were pinched from the library?"

"I'm sure they were."

"And some pages were taken from them relating to the last meningitis death?"

"Apparently."

"Any idea what was in the pages?"

"Just that they were doctor's records." Matthew outlined the rest of his conversation with Sister Murphy. "I like the idea that they were taken by relatives wanting to sue the hospital."

"A bit melodramatic," Geoffrey said. "Can you remember who else was in the library that morning?"

"Only the pharmacist, Mrs Swynnerton."

"She's very sensible. Why don't you ask her if she recalls anything odd?"

Helen ran Matthew back to the hospital after supper.

"Regards to your father," Geoffrey said as they shook hands. "Don't forget to ask Mrs Swynnerton if she saw anything unusual in the library."

They climbed into the car and Helen started the engine.

"And Matthew." Matthew wound down the window, and Geoffrey leant with his right arm on the roof to speak to him. "Don't forget to let me know."

CHAPTER TWENTY-THREE

Matthew liked Frances Swynnerton. She usually had a smile for him when they met around the hospital, and he had no hesitation in seeking her out in the pharmacy the day after supper at the Aylings. They sat down together in her office.

"I was talking to Sister Murphy yesterday," Matthew began.

Frances smiled. "Was that when you nearly banged into me in the Upper South corridor? You should never run in a hospital unless you're going to a cardiac arrest. It's supposed to be a restful place, not a rugby pitch."

"I'm sorry, but I was very late."

"Where were you rushing off to?"

"I was going to supper with a local farmer; he's a friend of my dad's."

"I know Geoffrey Ayling. He's on the hospital board."

"How did you know it was him?" Matthew was surprised.

"I guessed it was," Frances said after a moment. "He said he knew your father."

"Anyhow, Mr Ayling suggested I have a word with you." He told her how he thought the notes might have been taken from the library and how he'd tried to get them from records but they were booked out to Sister Murphy. "That's why I went to talk to her."

"You tried to get them! Why did you think you could do that? You're still only a medical student, Matthew."

She looked suddenly angry, and he explained nervously, "I suppose I shouldn't have done it, but I didn't like Dr Spence thinking I was that careless. And when he noticed pages were missing, I put two and two together."

"And?"

"I think somebody took the notes when I was at lunch so they could take the pages out."

"It sounds like a schoolboy fantasy to get you off the hook," she said unkindly, and Matthew flinched. "What did Sister Murphy make of it?"

"She said pages *were* missing, doctor's records, but she didn't know what was on them."

"The notes in this hospital are the worst I've ever come across. The filing's a disaster. Anyway, why did Geoffrey Ayling send you to me?"

"Because you were in the library that morning. Do you remember? It was only a couple of weeks ago. I was sitting at one of the window tables with the notes when you came in around midday. You said hello. I don't think you'd left when I went to get some lunch."

"Does Geoffrey Ayling think I took the notes?" Frances was incredulous.

"Of course he doesn't. He thinks you might remember if anybody else was there."

She thought hard. "Have you asked Anne Marsden, the librarian?"

"I saw her this morning. She was on leave that week."

She thought again. "Actually, I do think I remember you sitting by the window with a pile of notes."

"You asked me what I was doing," Matthew prompted.

"That's right. And you said you were going through the notes on meningitis patients. Then I saw you'd left them and gone to lunch." Matthew thought he was in for another lecture on confidentiality. "But I can only remember one other person there. I wonder why she didn't tell you herself."

"Not Daisy!" Matthew said, startled.

"Who's Daisy?"

"Daisy Thorpe. Student nurse."

Frances smiled. "Oh I see, your Daisy. No, it was Sister Murphy. She came in just after you left for lunch. I didn't take any notice of her after that, so I don't know what she did or how long she stayed, but she wasn't there for long, because I realised soon after that I was on my own again."

Matthew was flabbergasted. "Are you sure?"

"Of course I'm sure," Frances snapped. "Don't question me."

"But why didn't she say?"

"No idea. She's a funny woman sometimes. I should forget about it if I was you. I can't see you're going to get anywhere, and I can't believe it's important anyway."

***

Later that afternoon, Matthew met Geoffrey Ayling in the corridor on his way to a board meeting. He walked beside him.

"I've talked to Mrs Swynnerton. The only person she can remember in the library was Sister Murphy. She came in briefly just after I left for lunch.

Geoffrey stopped and stared at Matthew. "Is she sure?"

"Quite sure."

'And Sister Murphy didn't tell you that?'

Matthew shook his head.

"Did Mrs Swynnerton see her taking any notes?"

"She didn't notice what she did."

Geoffrey began to walk again. "Look, Matthew, I've got to rush. I'm late for the meeting. Thanks for letting me know."

"Do you want me to do anything else? Shall I talk to Sister Murphy again?"

Geoffrey stopped. "Don't do that on any account. You're not to mention it to her again. Do you understand?"

Matthew watched after him as he rushed off down the corridor.

***

After supper that evening Geoffrey took a large whisky to the study and sank into the comfortable leather armchair. He stared unseeingly at the mess of papers on his desk while he marshalled his thoughts. He'd had little doubt of Sister Murphy's guilt after the enquiry, now over a year ago, and he'd worried terribly that their hands had been tied through lack of evidence. Wendy Clarke had watched her very carefully, however, and he was sure there'd been no cause for anxiety. She had not given an intravenous drug herself since the enquiry, and she'd recently announced her intention to retire in a few months.

He couldn't understand why she had come to see him with the story about the syringes. That had been shortly before Jimmy died, and he had been uneasy about it ever since. If she was guilty, he'd have expected her to keep her head down after the enquiry, not come marching around to his house. But supposing she *was* innocent? Then it would have been perfectly reasonable for her to come. She didn't know what they thought the extra sterile water had been used for. She'd have been confused by their questions, wanting to sort it out for herself. Geoffrey realised that he'd tried to avoid confronting this possibility. If Sister Murphy hadn't killed the meningitis patients then either nobody had or, appallingly, somebody else was responsible, somebody they hadn't even begun to suspect. It was almost a relief, therefore, to be told today by Matthew that she was behaving oddly again. Presumably she had removed the notes from the library, taken out the missing pages, and then put the folder back on the desk in the afternoon for Matthew to find. But why did she get the notes out again after that? Had she altered something and now wanted to put the pages back? There must have been an entry in that folder that she didn't want Dr Spence to see, something in the doctor's notes.

He thought back to the enquiry. He remembered Jimmy describing the night he had found the scratches on the ampoule lids. Surely he would have recorded that in the notes. If he had done, Sister Murphy would have known, because she was there with him.

Oh Christ, he thought, reaching for the phone.

Wendy Clarke's number was ex-directory, and it took a while to persuade the hospital switchboard to give it to him.

"I'm sorry to call you so late, but it's important."

She listened carefully while he explained. "You think she didn't want Dr Spence to know about the marked ampoules?"

"That's what I'm afraid of. Is it possible she's using them again?"

Wendy reassured him. "Don't you remember? Jimmy told us at the enquiry that Frances had checked with the drug company and they'd explained that the scratches had been caused by a temporary fault in their crimping machine which they'd already corrected. The scratches were never significant."

"You're quite right," Geoffrey said. "I'd forgotten that. I'm sorry I bothered you so late, but I'm afraid I panicked a bit—I thought she was at it again."

"We never proved she was at it in the first place," she reminded him gently.

"Of course not. Why do you think Dr Spence wanted to see the notes on the meningitis patients anyway? It all happened a year before he came here."

"I wondered about that when you told me. I'll find out tomorrow, if you like, and call you back."

***

She rang before supper.

"Another one of your sisters," Fiona said, handing him the phone. "You seem to have quite a following! Don't be long."

He took the phone into his study.

"I asked Dr Spence why he wanted the notes," Wendy said. "They'd had another meningitis death, a young girl, and they were all upset by it, Matthew particularly. Simon thought it might help him to come to terms with it if he understood the condition better, so he asked him to draw the notes on the last half dozen or so cases at St Paul's. It was a teaching exercise."

"Simon Spence knows nothing about the enquiry?"

"I'm sure he doesn't. It was well before his time, and we kept it very secret, as you know."

"Could that be why she took the pages out? To stop him getting too interested?"

"It's a plausible explanation," Wendy said.

"Why would she get the notes out again later?"

"I imagine to put the pages back. She's been brought up to believe that hospital notes should never be interfered with. It's a big medico legal thing. She only intended to borrow the pages, not to take them permanently."

Geoffrey sighed. "I suppose it makes sense, but it's hardly how you'd expect a responsible person to behave. I take it she had nothing to do with this recent death?'

"The girl's name was Polly. She died on intensive care."

"She was never on Upper South?"

"No."

"So Sister Murphy wasn't involved at all?"

"She wasn't involved medically," Wendy said reluctantly.

"Do you mean she was involved in some other way?"

"She's a close friend of the family. She'd known Polly all her life. She sat with her parents all through the night, and she was in and around intensive care all through her illness. Polly died the next afternoon."

Geoffrey was silent for some time.
"Oh shit," he said eventually.

CHAPTER TWENTY-FOUR

Matthew collected Daisy from the nurses' home in his resurrected battered sports car. It was the evening after his meeting with Frances Swynnerton. They drove to The Lifeboatman pub in Massingham village, a mile from the beach. Matthew bought the drinks, a pint of Adnams for himself and a half of lager for Daisy. He had a fish pie and Daisy ordered scampi and chips.

"How did you get on with Sister Murphy?" she asked when they were settled in the smuggler's snug.

Matthew put his hand on the top of her thigh, under cover of the table.

Daisy giggled. "Not here Matthew!" She took his hand away.

"Maybe later?"

"We'll see."

He relaxed happily and sipped his beer. "It wasn't too bad. She was a bit funny at first, trying to pretend it was all nonsense and that I was just looking for an excuse for losing the notes. But then she asked me if I'd talked to anyone else, and I could see she was relieved when I said no, so I thought she probably knew something."

"She doesn't know we talked about it?"

He shook his head. "I didn't want her giving you a bad time on my account."

"My hero," Daisy said fondly.

"Anyhow, when I told her I knew she'd taken the notes out again, she changed completely and told me pages were missing and eventually she seemed to agree they might have been nicked from the library."

"So you were right after all!"

"I even gave her an idea why the pages had been removed: the relatives stole them so that eventually, when they sue the hospital, the missing pages will look like a cover-up."

"Wow! So somebody must have been watching you in the library."

"She gave me a cup of coffee," Matthew said smugly.

"I *am* impressed. I'm her favourite student and I've never had coffee! Who was in the library with you?"

He took a sip of Adnams. "Frances Swynnerton is the only one I remember."

"The pharmacy lady? I noticed her on the ward when you were in with Sister Murphy. She spent for ever fiddling around with the drug trolley outside the office and then she suddenly rushed off and left it with the lid open, just before you came out."

"I nearly banged into her in the corridor."

"Then Sister Murphy came out and found the lid open and went ballistic with the nurses but it wasn't our fault. I told her Mrs Swynnerton had been at the trolley most of the afternoon and she stared at me for ages. She's strange sometimes."

"I like her, but she can be odd," Matthew agreed. "She tried to get me to remember who'd been in the library that morning and completely forgot she'd been there herself."

Daisy giggled and the food arrived. They ate in concentrated silence. Matthew pinched the last of Daisy's chips and went to the bar for another round.

"You've got that wrong," she said when he returned. "Sister Murphy can't have been in the library—she was on the ward with me."

"She wasn't there long. Mrs Swynnerton said she saw her. She came in just after I left for lunch."

"She can't have done, Matthew," Daisy said firmly. "She was with me. That was the day of my ward assessment. It began at eleven. We did ward work for an hour and then we did the twelve o'clock drug round together. I sorted the medicines and she supervised me. That took another hour. Then we went to her office together to write up my ward book. We'd both got sandwiches from the canteen earlier, so we had a working lunch, and then she watched me get everything ready for Dr Spence's two o'clock ward round, which began on the dot as usual. Except you were late, of course."

"She must have slipped away occasionally to do other things."

"She never does." Daisy was adamant. "She takes ward assessments very seriously. I'm absolutely certain she was with me all the time."

"Oh God," Matthew groaned. "So now Mrs Swynnerton is the one who's confused. I wish I'd never started this, Daisy! Mr Ayling seemed to think it was important when I told him Sister Murphy was in the library, and now I'll have to tell him she wasn't. Half an hour late for supper and now this! He'll think I'm a complete twit."

"It's hardly your fault if Mrs Swynnerton gets her facts wrong."

"I suppose not." He put his hand on her thigh. "It's a warm night. Why don't we drive down to the beach when we've finished our drinks and see if that hut's empty?"

Daisy put her hand on his and smiled into his eyes. "We'll see."

CHAPTER TWENTY-FIVE

"Matthew phoned just after you went out," Fiona said. "I told him you'd be back around now. He said it was about your friend Sister Murphy."

Geoffrey went into the study and sat at his desk. It was his paperwork afternoon—management, he supposed they'd call it in the hospital. Fiona bought him a cup of tea and a cheese sandwich.

"You get a sort of hunted look when that woman's name is mentioned."

He grinned. "It's a miracle I don't fall to the ground in a dead faint. I'll tell you about it one day."

He tried to concentrate on his papers but couldn't get his mind off Matthew's call, and it was a relief when the phone rang. He listened carefully.

"Is your Daisy quite certain she never left the ward?"

"She was with her all the time."

"And she's sure she's got the right day?"

"I asked her to check the date in the ward book. It's signed by Sister Murphy at one thirty p.m., exactly when Mrs Swynnerton saw her in the library."

"So Mrs Swynnerton *can't* have seen her. Did she seem quite certain about it when she told you she had?"

"Absolutely. I was so surprised that Sister Murphy seemed to have forgotten she'd been there herself that I asked Mrs Swynnerton if she was sure, and she got quite cross with me for questioning her."

Geoffrey thought hard. "All right, Matthew. I think we'll have to leave it there. Everybody seems to be confused about what really happened, and it's probably not important anyway. Let's forget about it."

"Might be best if I don't leave notes lying around in the library?" Geoffrey smiled. "Might be."

He got no work done that afternoon, and when Fiona bought him a cup of tea later, the mess on his desk looked exactly the same. After supper he sat in his office until midnight. He had only recently begun to suspect that there might be a jigsaw, and as the evening went on, he realised that now he had many of the pieces. But they wouldn't make the picture he wanted them to. There was only one way they would fit together perfectly, and the image they created appalled him.

The day after Matthew's phone call, Geoffrey arranged a meeting with Celia Willoughby, his fellow non-executive director, and Wendy Clarke. They met in Wendy's office at five o'clock.

"Bit of a squash I'm afraid," she said, handing out tea and looking curiously at Geoffrey as he squeezed himself into the chintzy chair. He'd wanted the meeting urgently but wouldn't explain why.

Celia waited patiently.

"I think we may have a serious problem on our hands," Geoffrey began. "We're going to have to bring it to the chief executive, but I thought we should meet like this first and get things absolutely clear in our own minds before he contributes his own particular brand of confusion to the subject."

Celia grinned; Farrell's performance on the board had been increasingly erratic lately, and she and Geoffrey both felt that he was finding it increasingly hard to resist the call of the real world of garden furniture.

"It's about the meningitis deaths."

"She's not at it again?" Celia said, aghast. "I thought we were watching her carefully."

"Sister Murphy's not at it again. She never was. I think we've made a terrible mistake. She could no more harm a patient than she could fly to the moon."

"Have you found something that definitely proves she couldn't have done it?" Celia said impatiently.

"It's more than that. I think we've been watching the wrong person, and another patient has died because of it."

The two women put their tea cups down with a clatter. Wendy spoke first. "Are you saying the meningitis patients *were* killed but not by Sister Murphy?"

"And whoever killed them has killed somebody else?" Celia was shocked. "Geoffrey, this is terrible. Do you really know what you're saying?"

"All the evidence against her was circumstantial. She was only behaving like an old-fashioned sister would. The union chap, Tony Parsons, confirmed that. The hospital is her life. It was nothing to her to come in after hours to give injections."

"But she gave them all herself!"

"Her instinct told her something was wrong but she didn't know what it was. She distrusts the way student nurses are taught and thought it was safest to give the injections herself. There's nothing more to it than that."

"But she must have used all that extra sterile water for something."

Geoffrey looked at Wendy. "Did we ever check that Upper South really had used more sterile water that month?"

"We didn't have to. Frances Swynnerton confirmed it at the enquiry."

"She didn't confirm it—she *told* us. That was the first time anybody had heard about it. We only have her word for it." He told them about Sister Murphy's visit to his house almost a year ago. "She pointed out that if they'd used more sterile water they should have used more syringes, but they hadn't. She had the documents from supplies to prove it."

"But why would Mrs Swynnerton bother to mislead us about something like that?" Celia said. "You're not making sense to me, Geoffrey."

"Perhaps she wanted us to believe in Sister Murphy's guilt."

"Why on earth would she want that?"

The two women stared at him while he told how Doctor Spence had found that pages were missing from the meningitis notes, and about Matthew's conviction that the notes had been taken while he was at lunch and the pages removed. He explained how Frances Swynnerton had lied, insisting that Sister Murphy was in the library when she could not possibly have been there.

"She thought Sister Murphy was in the library when she wasn't!" Celia shook her head. "That's not a lie, Geoffrey, it's a mistake. It was two weeks ago, for heaven's sake."

"I believe it was a deliberate attempt to mislead us. She wanted me to believe that Sister Murphy had removed the pages from the notes when in fact she had done it herself."

"Do you know what was on the pages?"

"I think it was Jimmy Greenhalgh's comments about the scratches on the ampoules."

"So why did Sister Murphy get the notes out again after they'd been returned to records?" Wendy asked.

"She wanted to see which pages were missing, although I expect she had already guessed." He looked at the two women. "I think Sister Murphy and I are following the same trail."

"Well, you're a lot further along it than I am," Celia said.

They were all silent for a while, marshalling their thoughts.

Wendy spoke first. "Do you think Frances Swynnerton took the notes and removed the pages?"

Geoffrey nodded.

"But why?" Celia said, exasperated. "Why should she care if Dr Spence found out about the enquiry?"

"She wasn't worried about that. Look, Celia, I lay awake all night thinking about this. I've been over it all in my mind a hundred times trying to find a different explanation for the facts, but I always arrive at the same conclusion. Just listen to me now. Frances Swynnerton took the pages from the notes because she didn't want anybody to read about the marked ampoules."

Wendy made to interrupt, and he raised his hand. "Listen. She hadn't expected the notes of a dead patient to resurface, but when they did she had to act quickly. She didn't want Dr Spence reading about the scratches on the ampoule lids."

Wendy interrupted again, and this time he couldn't stop her. "But we went through this the other day, Geoffrey. The lids were scratched on the production line. It was sorted out at the time."

"And whose word do we have for that?"

"You mean it didn't happen in the factory?"

"I don't think she ever contacted the drug company."

"Why wouldn't she?" Celia asked.

"Because the marked ampoules were hers. She produced them. It's her machine that marks the lids. And she certainly wouldn't want anybody analysing the contents. Whatever they contained it wasn't penicillin."

"Oh Christ," Celia said. "Now I see what you're getting at."

Nobody spoke for several minutes.

Eventually, Celia broke the silence. "You said earlier on that another patient might have died. Surely not?"

"There's been another meningitis death, a girl called Polly. I asked Matthew about it. He was quite involved. He said she got a lot better during the night, so much so that he left intensive care in the morning thinking she was going to recover. Polly went downhill quickly after that, and she was dead by the afternoon."

"How old was she?" Celia whispered.

"Eighteen," Wendy said.

"Just go through it again, Geoffrey," Celia said. "Tell us exactly what you think's been going on."

"Frances Swynnerton killed the meningitis patients by interfering with the penicillin. She might have got away with it if Jimmy hadn't noticed the marks on the ampoules. She must have her own capping machine. I would guess that she fills old penicillin ampoules that she's got from pharmacy waste with something useless, maybe even poisonous, caps them and substitutes them for the real penicillin on the ward. She pretended she'd contacted the drug company so we all believed there was nothing wrong with the penicillin, and she tried to divert attention from herself by suggesting it was Sister Murphy who was mad."

"That's right," Wendy agreed. "I remember Jimmy saying it was her who first planted the seed in his mind."

"Sister Murphy played into her hands, of course, by insisting on giving the injections herself. The sterile water story was brilliant. I'm sure Upper South used no more that month than any other, but it gave the enquiry a solid core to spin its fantasies about. We believed exactly what she wanted us to! Then it sounds as though Jimmy began to get suspicious about whether she had actually contacted the drug company. That's when he asked Wendy to make some enquiries, but it came to nothing because a few days later, he was dead."

Celia looked up at Geoffrey. "That can't be a coincidence, can it?"

"I don't know. He was a big man. She couldn't have got him to the wreck and killed him herself, and I doubt if she's got accomplices. Whatever happened to Jimmy, once he was out of the way the heat was off. Presumably there were no more suspicious deaths until Polly?"

"I'm not aware of any," Wendy said

"And then Simon Spence asked for the notes on the meningitis patients."

There was a shocked silence for several minutes.

"You've no proof of any of this, have you?" Celia said hopefully.

"Not so far. We can't do anything until we get it, but it shouldn't be difficult. We need to talk to the medical officer of the drug company—Wendy knows which one. I'll do that first thing tomorrow.

And we need to get the pharmacy records and see if Upper South really did use extra sterile water in March. Can we do that tonight without Mrs Swynnerton knowing?"

"I'll find a way," Wendy said.

"Can you also find out if there's anybody on the wards who isn't responding to penicillin as they should, and if so get one of the ampoules? Mrs Swynnerton must realise that Sister Murphy is onto her after the business with the notes, so she won't be using marked ampoules now. She'll have got herself another crimper. We need to get the contents of a ward ampoule analysed."

They agreed to meet again next morning at ten o'clock. Wendy left, and Celia and Geoffrey sat for a time in silence.

"You think you're right, don't you, Geoffrey?"

"I'm afraid so. What about you?"

"You might be right," she admitted sadly. "How are we going to live with this? We've let a mad woman make fools of us, and an eighteen-year-old girl has died as a consequence." Her eyes filled with tears.

CHAPTER TWENTY-SIX

Finoula Murphy posted a long letter to her cousin Sean on his Connemara island and was in bed by nine o'clock. She'd been sleeping badly lately. She tried to avoid sleeping tablets, but she'd needed them around the time of the enquiry, and they'd worked then, so she'd got another prescription from Simon Spence's registrar. She'd taken it to the hospital pharmacy that morning and collected the bottle of tablets in a sealed white paper bag when she finished work in the evening. The label on the bottle said that twenty pills had been dispensed, but there were only two when she opened it. *Enough for tonight,* she thought. She'd sort it out with pharmacy in the morning. She swallowed both of them and climbed into bed.

She was dozing within a few minutes. *These ones work well,* she thought, beginning to remember Dr Greenhalgh's death, as she often did before sleep. Sean wouldn't admit he'd done it, but of course he had. You'd need at least two strong men to drag him to the wreck and he had plenty of those. She'd tried many times to calm him down, but he wouldn't listen.

She thought of Inishbaron and the Mweelrea mountain, of the cottage and her mother. She would go back there soon for good, to look after Michael. She saw him now, lying on his bed in the small back room, looking through the red-framed window at the thorn tree on the stony slope, dreaming of his father's arms about him.

Within a few minutes, she was asleep and her mind emptied of thought.

CHAPTER TWENTY-SEVEN

They met next morning in Wendy's office at ten o'clock.

"Unfortunately, Rowan Heath is away at a meeting until next week," Geoffrey said. "He's the medical officer of the company that supplies all our penicillin. He's on a family hiking holiday in Italy and apparently uncontactable. I talked to his deputy, but he's only been in post for a few months and has no knowledge of any of this."

"I checked with the assistant pharmacist," Wendy said. "They only keep records of sterile water usage for two months. It's a system Mrs Swynnerton introduced last year to save space."

"What a surprise. Did you find out if anybody on the wards isn't responding to penicillin as they should?"

"There is somebody, I'm afraid."

"Oh no." Celia leant forward, alarmed.

"Mr Raspberry on Upper South, Dr Spence's patient. He's got bacterial endocarditis and he's not responding to the antibiotics. This is an ampoule from the ward." She held it up. "There's no mark on the lid, but that means nothing. She'd have been too careful to have gone on using the same crimping machine. We'll get the contents analysed."

Wendy's bleep sounded. "I'll have to take it, I'm afraid; it's the urgent tone."

She called the switchboard, who put her straight through to Eileen Kenny, Finoula Murphy's friend.

"My God," she said.

Geoffrey looked up sharply. "Is something wrong?"

She stared at him, concentrating on the voice on the phone, her face pale. "All right, Eileen. Stay calm. I'm coming now."

"What's happened?" Geoffrey said quietly.

Her hand was shaking when she put the phone down.

"That was Eileen Kenny, Finoula's housemate. She didn't come to work, so Eileen went back to the house to see if she was all right. She found her dead in bed with an empty bottle of sleeping pills beside her."

CHAPTER TWENTY-EIGHT

Detective Sergeant Hicks stood in the small bedroom and stared down at Sister Murphy's body. She appeared to be peacefully asleep in the single bed. The sheets were undisturbed. He examined the empty pill bottle on the bedside table. The label confirmed that twenty sleeping tablets had been dispensed the day before by the pharmacy at St Paul's. A large glass of water on the table was almost empty. He sipped it—just water. There was no note.

Wendy Thorpe waited for him with Geoffrey and Celia in the trust boardroom. The chief executive was on leave, but Wendy had contacted him and he agreed that now the police should be involved.

"It looks pretty straightforward to me," Hicks said when he was shown in by one of the porters. "Is there something else I should know?"

"Quite a lot, I'm afraid," Wendy said.

Hicks listened while she told of the enquiry into Sister Murphy's actions after the unexpected meningitis deaths.

"You didn't involve us then?"

"We were very concerned, but there really was no firm evidence that she was anything other than a conscientious ward sister. It would have been impossible to keep a police enquiry secret and her life would have been destroyed. We decided to watch her closely, and she was banned from giving intravenous injections herself."

"And?"

"And nothing, really. We were actually beginning to wonder if another member of staff might have been involved."

"So why do you think she killed herself?"

"Guilt, maybe. Perhaps she couldn't live any longer with the knowledge of what she'd done."

"No new evidence has surfaced against her that she might have been aware of?" Hicks asked.

Wendy shook her head.

"Could she have known that yesterday we took an ampoule of penicillin from her ward for analysis?" Geoffrey asked.

"I suppose she could," Wendy said. "I hadn't thought of that."

"Why did you do that?" Hicks asked.

"We were concerned about a patient on her ward. He had a serious condition that should have responded to penicillin, but he was deteriorating"

"And she might have been interfering with the medication?"

"Her or somebody else."

"Let's stick with her for the moment. We need to look around the house."

"Don't you need a warrant?"

"Not if an owner consents. I believe she shares the house with another sister?"

"She's joint owner of the house with her friend Eileen Kenny. I've never been there but I've heard that they've divided the property so they each live in part of it."

Back at the house, the uniformed policewoman who had stayed with Eileen explained to her that a search of Finoula's side of the house might help explain her suicide. Eileen agreed.

Her friend's death had stunned her. As far as she knew, Finoula was happily looking forward to retiring in a few months and returning to Connemara to look after Michael.

Hicks phoned a colleague and left to join him at the house. Wendy, Geoffrey and Celia arranged to meet him back in the boardroom at 3 p.m., but he phoned just after midday and asked to meet again at once.

He laid out four transparent evidence bags on the boardroom table. "We found three of these in her side of the kitchen. She has her own units and her own small fridge."

The first bag contained a dozen empty drug ampoules, labelled as penicillin and uncapped.

"These were hidden in the middle of a pile of tea towels in a drawer on her side of the sink."

The second bag contained an opened packet of granulated sugar.

"Except it's not granulated sugar," Hicks said. "It's a flat white powder. We found it at the back of her food cupboard behind two real packets of sugar."

The third largest bag contained a heavy instrument like a big stapler, about a foot long. With it was a packet of ampoule caps. Without opening the transparent bag, Hicks pointed out how a cap could be fitted into the jaws of the instrument and then forced down onto an ampoule with the long handle. It was a portable crimping machine.

Wendy and the two non-executive directors sat in shocked silence.

"There was no note," Hicks said, "but I suppose there was no need for one. She must have known we'd find this lot. Perhaps it was her way of confessing."

"She's out of it," Geoffrey said, "but she's made sure we won't be when it gets out that we seriously suspected her six months ago and let her go on working."

"You don't think she's killed again in the meantime?"

They told him about Polly's unexpected death and how Sister Murphy had sat with her throughout her illness.

"My God," Hicks said. "Then there's this." He opened the fourth bag, which contained a rolled bundle of papers, held together with an elastic band. "These are letters, all from a bloke called Sean Murphy. They are well thumbed and look as though they've been read time and again. They were in her bedside locker. I've read a few, and they're affectionate but not sexy."

"And?" Wendy said.

"The letters were postmarked Westport, which is in the west of Ireland. He mentions a Ned Fogarty and a ship called the *Queen of the Isles*. My colleagues back at the station have talked to the officers in Westport. Fogarty is skipper of a ferry boat which serves some of the offshore islands. Inishbaron is one of those islands. Sean Murphy is one of the few inhabitants. He has strong IRA connections. The letters refer almost obsessively to Jimmy Greenhalgh. Sean is obviously aware of the enquiry into Sister Murphy but apparently not aware of her guilt. He blames Dr Greenhalgh for the whole thing. Several times he mentions Priest's Rock. It's in the harbour of Inishbaron. Oliver Cromwell once chained a cleric to it and left him to drown in the incoming tide."

***

Any suspicions about Frances Swynnerton had vanished with the proof of Sister Murphy's guilt, and Geoffrey could see no reason to phone the medical director of the drug company when it was confirmed that the ampoule sent for analysis contained only lactose. St Paul's, of course, was in turmoil, and became the focus of a national scandal: a hospital enquiry exonerating a killer who went on to kill again. The Trust Board was disbanded and an interim chief executive and board appointed. Farrell, who persistently maintained that the enquiry had acted against his wishes, left with a generous severance payout, resigned from the NHS and returned to his previous life. Geoffrey and Celia, the two non-executive directors on the original panel, were subjected to a vicious media attack, as were Colin Smythe and Tony Parsons, the union representatives. Wendy, too devastated to continue working, had resigned at once and somehow managed to avoid the press, although the formal enquiry a year later would criticise all of them severely.

Eileen Kenny, Finoula's housemate, put the house on the market and returned to Connemara. She gave Finoula's share of the sale to her mother to help with Michael's care.

Detective Sergeant Hicks and his Irish colleagues were unable to establish a connection between Sean Murphy and Jimmy's death.

PART FOUR:

OCTOBER 1995

ONE MONTH BEFORE JIMMY'S DEATH

CHAPTER TWENTY-NINE

Two evenings after the enquiry, Jimmy and Frances lay entwined in a double sleeping bag in *Felicity*'s cabin. The evenings were drawing in, and the cabin heater was temperamental.

"We'll have to use my cottage," Frances said. "You can park behind the pub and take the path on the edge of the marsh. Nobody will see you."

He nuzzled her neck sleepily. "You're sure about those sterile water deliveries to Upper South?"

She sat up angrily. "You know I've checked. Do you want to see the papers yourself?"

"Of course not," Jimmy said.

She was furious when he asked her again about the sterile water two weeks later, after Sister Murphy's visit to Geoffrey Ayling's house.

"Come and see the bloody records," she shouted. "You're suggesting I lied!"

"Calm down." He was irritated.

Felicity was definitely too cold now and they had begun to meet in Frances' cottage. He had driven there for a quick lunch at her suggestion but he couldn't relax. He worried that his car would be recognised and felt he was too old to creep around the marshes at the back.

"Come on," she had said when he tapped on the kitchen door. "Screw first, lunch after."

Sex wasn't a success. A long morning in the clinic wasn't the best aphrodisiac, and Jimmy was finding at this stage of his affair with Frances that he needed all the help he could get. He was beginning to dwell on flaws that at first he had found touching: the large mole on her cheek, the way her gums retracted above her upper teeth when she smiled.

"Calm down. I only want to talk about it, and there's not many people I can talk to. I'm worried that she'd go to Geoffrey Ayling's house like that. You'd think she'd want to keep her head down with the enquiry over and no blame attached to her. If she was guilty, that is."

"She's guilty as hell" Frances said angrily. "I watch her like a hawk, but nutters like her are devious. I can't believe what you did at the enquiry."

"We had no choice," Jimmy said wearily. They'd been over it many times.

CHAPTER THIRTY

The *Fenlander* was a pretentious name for the rattling old banger he was travelling in, but Jimmy settled back happily in his seat after Littleport and waited for the first view of Ely Cathedral, its huge bulk and buttresses perfectly framed in the distance by the ponds and willows of the fen. The rest of the trip was sheer tedium. After Cambridge, the *Fenlander* became a commuter train, increasingly packed and uncomfortable as it approached King's Cross station. He waited until the carriage was empty before he pulled himself stiffly out of his seat and walked through the modern concourse to the taxi rank.

"College of Physicians, please."

The driver stared at him silently and Jimmy climbed in, waiting for the usual reluctant admission.

The window slid back. "Isn't that the one in Camberwell, squire?"

"No, just down the road in Regent's Park."

They crawled through traffic for several minutes before the driver turned again. "North side, squire, innit?"

"No. It's just round the corner. Drop me off here please."

The cabbie accepted his tip graciously and Jimmy crossed the busy Euston Road and walked the remaining few hundred yards. He stood at the edge of the park and stared at the college with his usual disbelief. Thick slabs of soiled angular grey concrete piled higgledy-piggledy made an astonishing end to a perfect Nash terrace. If he were the taxi driver he'd probably try to forget it too, he thought, pushing through the heavy glass doors, but it was comfortable inside.

The Advanced Medicine course each autumn provided a welcome break from the repetitive tedium of clinics and ward rounds, and a chance to catch up with old friends. Angela always came as well and they stayed at the Langham Hotel in Upper Regent Street, within easy walking distance. She would be down on a later train.

He sat on occasional College committees, and the porter recognised him and smiled a welcome. He pinned his label to his jacket, descended the stairs to the concourse and collected a cup of coffee, looking around the room for familiar faces. A friend from medical school came across.

"Here we are again. Is Angela coming down?"

Groups formed and dissolved, past friends and acquaintances meeting again and moving on. Eventually he found himself talking to somebody he didn't recognise. They introduced themselves, and he saw that Peter Willis worked at Frenchams. The hospital name was familiar but he couldn't think why, and soon they moved through to the hall for the first lecture. Later in the day, in the middle of a boring session, he remembered that Frenchams was the hospital in the Midlands where Frances had worked before she came to St Paul's. A few months ago he would have thought about her with pleasure and excitement, but now his predominant feeling was guilt. He was looking forward to seeing Angela that evening.

He met Peter Willis at lunch next day. "I knew I'd heard the name of your hospital recently but I couldn't remember why."

"And you have now?"

"We pinched your senior pharmacist. She'd worked at Frenchams for several years and then her husband died and she decided she needed a change."

"Frances Swynnerton!"

"That's right; they hadn't been married long when he was killed in a car crash."

Willis looked at him in surprise. "You've got that bit wrong, I think."

"I'm sure she said a car crash."

"I know how he died because he died on my ward. He had lobar pneumonia."

"Following the crash?"

"There wasn't a crash." Willis thought for a moment. "He was admitted with pneumonia and we grew a pneumococcus from his blood. He was a fit man in his middle forties, so I couldn't understand why he died."

"It wasn't a resistant bug?"

"There aren't many penicillin-resistant pneumococci around, as you know. But this one was definitely sensitive."

"I suppose it happens," Jimmy said.

"I suppose so. We flooded him with antibiotics but he just got worse and worse. We moved him to intensive care when he developed septic shock, but nothing made the slightest difference—the infection overwhelmed him. It was very traumatic, of course, with his wife working in the hospital. He took a while to die. She was devastated."

"I think she said they hadn't been married long?"

"Not long. He was a local solicitor. I knew him vaguely. Nice chap."

The college provided an excellent buffet lunch, and they chewed happily for a while.

"She's an attractive woman," Willis said, glancing briefly at Jimmy. "Has she got a local beau?"

"I'm not sure."

"You want to watch out! She's a doctor groupie! I was surprised when she married a solicitor."

Jimmy concentrated on peeling his king prawn.

That evening, he ate alone with Angela in the Langham Hotel. *We've been together a long time,* he thought. He watched her hands as she ate, puffed and freckled with the spots of age, and knew that he had never stopped loving her.

CHAPTER THIRTY-ONE

Why would Frances lie to him? Jimmy wondered, as he rattled back from London on the *Fenlander*. What difference could it make how her husband died? The more he thought about it the less sense it made and the more he realised that he didn't really care. By the time they got to Cambridge he was bored with the subject, and when they reached Market Houghton his thoughts were happily with Angela again. He considered confronting Frances but quickly thought the better of it; he was beginning to realise how nasty her temper could be.

Every Friday lunchtime, a meeting was held in the Postgraduate Centre for the hospital doctors and any general practitioners who were able to come. Lunch was followed by a lecture, usually given by an invited speaker from elsewhere. Two weeks after his return from London, Jimmy bought his junior doctors down to the centre at the end of his morning ward round. Mr Vass had been admitted and they had diagnosed sub-acute bacterial endocarditis. It was four weeks before Jimmy's death at the wreck.

He was particularly keen to hear today's speaker, the medical director of a large drug company. There was a complex relationship between the pharmaceutical industry and the medical profession. Doctors liked to believe that they were independent in their use of drugs, but the companies knew better and devoted huge resources to monitoring their prescribing habits. There were strict rules about gifts to doctors but there were ways around this, usually under the guise of further education. Few doctors travelled to meetings abroad without financial help from the industry, and most postgraduate activity—today's meeting for example—was heavily subsidised. Nobody paid for lunch.

It was a frank and informative talk. They heard how the drug companies had a file on every doctor in the country, his prescribing habits and his views on the industry. Would he talk to drug reps, did he accept money for research, did he like to go to meetings in Australia? The medical director might work for the drug company but he was still a doctor at heart and his message was simple—there's no such thing as a free lunch. Jimmy hoped that the junior doctors understood.

"I enjoyed that very much." He was drinking coffee with Rowan Heath, the speaker, in the anteroom to the lecture theatre. "I've often wondered if your job would be more interesting than mine."

Rowan grinned. "Better paid, I expect."

"How long have you been with them?

"Several years. Long enough. I'm moving on soon."

"I wondered why you were so frank! It must have been you who dealt with our enquiries about the quality of your penicillin earlier this year."

Rowan thought. "Something like that should have come to me, certainly," he agreed, "but I can't say I remember it. Perhaps I was away at the time. I'm out of the office a lot these days, so my deputy might have handled it. What was it about?"

Jimmy told him about the scratched ampoules and his anxieties about the antibiotics. He explained how Frances had contacted the medical officer, presumably Rowan's deputy, and how the marks had been traced to a fault in their crimping machine. The pharmacy had sent ampoules back, which the drug company had checked, and the penicillin was pure. They'd carried out an extensive review of the production process and quality control and found nothing wrong.

"All news to me," Rowan said. "I wouldn't normally forget something like that. Much more interesting than what I usually get up to. Anyhow, I'm glad it was all sorted out."

He left to drive to a meeting in Norwich, and Jimmy finished his coffee. Frances had also attended the lecture and he noticed her now across the anteroom, watching him. He smiled at her but she didn't smile back.

Rowan called a week later. He remembered their conversation and was puzzled by it. Doubts were rarely expressed about the purity of a drug, at least in this country, and he should have been informed at once. His deputy was away until Thursday but he had arranged a meeting with him immediately on his return.

"It's very odd. We just have no record of it at all. Are you sure it was our penicillin?"

"I thought it was, but I suppose it can't have been. I'm sorry to have put you to the trouble."

"No problem at all," Rowan said.

***

Angela was away at her parents for a few days and Jimmy reluctantly stayed the night in Frances' cottage. It was the first time they had met since the lecture.

"You were talking to Rowan Heath for a long time," she said over supper. "What was that about?"

"I told him I'd enjoyed his talk. I'm glad someone who works for a drug company is honest enough to put that message across."

Frances smiled. "I'm surprised they don't get rid of him." She sipped some more wine. "Is that all you talked about?"

"No. I think I made a bit of a fool of myself, actually. I thought we got our penicillin from his company and I thanked him for his help in March. It was news to him, and he phoned this morning to say I'd got the wrong company. It was nice of him to follow it up and get back to me."

Frances stared at him in silence for a long time, and he became uneasy.

Her face contorted suddenly and she jumped up, knocking over her wine glass. "You bastard," she snarled. "You were checking up on me again!"

Jimmy was shocked. "Checking up on you?"

"Just like you did with the sterile water and those bloody syringes. You're beginning to believe that fucking bitch Finoula Murphy."

She picked up her fallen wine glass and threw it hard at him across the table. He moved, but it clipped his cheek, and there was blood on his finger when he touched the spot.

"For Christ's sake, Frances, sit down and shut up. I'm leaving now."

"How dare you listen to that bitch. How dare you check up on what I've told you."

"I'm not checking up on you," he shouted. "But perhaps I should. You're not as honest as you pretend to be."

She leant across the table. "What the hell do you mean?"

Jimmy didn't want this, but he was very angry. "I know you lied about your husband."

She was suddenly still. "Lied about him?"

"He didn't die in a car crash, did he, Frances?"

"How did he die then?"

"Pneumonia. If you can tell a pointless lie like that, I reckon you can lie about anything."

"How dare you!" she screamed. "How dare you dig into my life."

She grabbed the second glass and threw it at him, missing this time but splashing him with claret.

"Which drug company was it, Frances?" he taunted her. "Tell me so I can give their medical officer a call."

"Get out of my cottage."

"Which company, Frances?"

"Mind your own fucking business."

He was suddenly sick of it all. His anger subsided.

"Oh sod off," he said wearily. "I'm leaving. You're a weird woman, Frances. I wish we'd never met."

"Me too," she shouted. "You're a boring old fart and fucking useless in bed. Get out of here and don't ever come back. And just remember: if I find you've been checking up on me again, I'll make sure the whole hospital knows all about us. I'll make sure they know what a rotten lover you are, although I don't suppose *that* will be any surprise to Angela."

"Sod off," Jimmy said again.

As he closed the door, he heard the wine bottle smash against it.

CHAPTER THIRTY-TWO

Jimmy was becoming increasingly concerned about David Vass, his patient with bacterial endocarditis. Despite three weeks of intravenous penicillin, there was no sign that he was responding to antibiotics. His temperature should have settled quickly, but it was still there, the low-grade fever produced by an infected heart valve. He had reviewed the blood cultures with Anthony Cosgrove, the bacteriologist.

"Typical Strep viridans," Anthony said, showing him the petri dishes and pointing out the green halo around the colonies of bacteria. "Nothing funny about it at all."

"And penicillin sensitive?"

"Very."

They looked at the dishes containing the discs of blotting paper soaked in penicillin. No colonies grew near them.

"He's been in three weeks now and he's no better."

"Are you giving him gentamicin as well?"

"Right from the start. The blood levels are in the correct range, so the dose is right. And we're flooding him with penicillin."

"They don't always do well."

"But this chap should. Only sixty-three, previously very fit, aortic valve affected by rheumatic fever when he was a child but only slightly damaged. Everything's in his favour. I suppose there's no point in further blood cultures?"

"Not really. There'll be no bacteria alive in his blood with all that penicillin swilling around. They're snuggled away in crevices in the valve."

He met Angus Wilson, the pathologist, in the covered way between the pathology labs and the main hospital. It was a while since they had talked. Jimmy had tended to avoid his friends, feeling increasingly guilty about his relationship with Frances. Angus in turn had sensed that something was wrong. He and Mary had discussed it but had no idea what the problem was.

He invited Jimmy to his office for coffee. Angus sat on the high stool in front of his microscope, and Jimmy took the chair behind the desk looking out over the birch wood.

"Why are you down in the labs?" Angus asked.

He listened while Jimmy explained his worries about Mr Vass.

"Perhaps your Sister Murphy's at it again," he said with a grin. "Did anything ever come of that business with the meningitis cases? I remember you were worried that she was misbehaving. Wasn't there some sort of enquiry?"

"There was nothing in it."

Angus looked affectionately at his old friend. "You and Angela must come round to supper soon."

When he was back in his own office, he bleeped Wendy Clarke. "I know you've been keeping a close eye on Sister Murphy," he said. "I suppose there's no possibility she's fiddling with Mr Vass' medication? He's the endocarditis case on Upper South."

"None at all. She never gives intravenous drugs, not since the enquiry."

It was now three weeks since Jimmy's meeting in the Postgraduate Centre with Rowan Heath, two weeks since his row with Frances, and just one week until his death at the wreck. He hadn't seen her again. They avoided each other in the hospital, and as far as he was concerned, their affair was finished. But he didn't want to upset her now he knew how volatile she could be. He was sure she'd carry out her threat to let the hospital know of their affair, no doubt with lots of detail, real and imagined. He couldn't bear the thought of Angela hearing about it like that. He hadn't tried to check which company had provided the penicillin. Frances might find out about his enquiries, and he'd managed to persuade himself it was a pointless exercise anyway. He wasn't too pleased, therefore, when his secretary told him that Rowan Heath was trying to contact him again. He left it until after the weekend and might have left it altogether if Rowan hadn't phoned again on Monday evening and caught him at the end of a clinic.

"I'm sorry to keep on about this, Jimmy. Did you ever find out who else was providing you with penicillin?"

"Sounds like industrial espionage."

Rowan laughed. "I suppose it does. But it's not, really. It's just that I've checked our order books and we do provide you with a lot on a regular basis. I can't believe you'd need any more. Did you find out where else it was coming from?"

"I'm afraid I forgot about it." He was not altogether truthful, remembering the force with which the claret bottle hit the door.

Rowan sounded disappointed. "Well, I just thought I'd let you know."

"Thanks for phoning," Jimmy said.

He bleeped Wendy Clarke. "Twice in one week!" she said. "Whatever next."

"Can you do something for me?" he asked. "I need to know the names of the drug companies who supply our penicillin."

"Why don't you ask Frances Swynnerton?"

"There's a very good reason why I can't. You'll have to trust me, Wendy. It's particularly important that she doesn't know."

"I'll find out; it shouldn't take long. But on one condition."

"Go on."

"That you tell me one day what it's all about."

Jimmy smiled. "Fair enough."

She had the information Jimmy wanted by lunchtime the following day. Frances was away until Friday and Wendy had talked to the assistant pharmacist.

"Why do you need to know?" he'd asked

"It's the School of Nursing," she said vaguely. "Some project the students are doing on the drug industry."

He showed her the penicillin on the shelves. "It all comes from the same company. They give us a very good deal. We haven't used anybody else for years."

Jimmy was in his private rooms when she called. He shared a Georgian house in the centre of town with several colleagues, and when his last patient had gone he stood by the window looking down at the market square. He watched the traders packing their unsold goods into vans, dismantling stalls and rolling up canopies. Occasionally in the past he'd gone down and bought fruit at a give-away price.

So Frances never contacted the drug company, he thought. She'd lied about that like she'd lied about her husband. Perhaps she'd also lied about the sterile water at the enquiry; it was odd that the ward hadn't needed more syringes. She seemed to have lied about everything. He sighed. He'd never had an affair before. If he hadn't bedded Frances none of this would have happened, or at least he wouldn't have known about it. She was a pathological liar with a filthy temper.

The more he tried to work it out, the more confused he became. What could Frances hope to gain from it all? Perhaps the memories of her husband's death were too painful for her. He could just about understand that. And perhaps there was some feud with Sister Murphy he didn't know about. At least that would explain the lie about the sterile water, if it was a lie. But the marked ampoules were different. She only had to make a phone call to the medical officer, for God's sake. And not only did she not make the call, she then pretended she had!

He shook his head. Whatever the explanation, he had got himself involved with a dangerous woman who could destroy his reputation and his marriage and make him a laughing stock in the hospital.

He walked across to the large oak desk and sat behind it. He shared this consulting room with one other colleague, who used the desk drawers on the left. Jimmy unlocked the top one on the right. The ampoule was still there, in a tray with paper clips, pencils and rubber bands. He'd found it in his suit a few days after he'd noticed the scratches with Sister Murphy that evening on Upper South. He must have dropped it in his pocket and forgotten about it. He took off his glasses and examined the scratch again. It might have been significant, particularly since they were so worried about the meningitis deaths. It was negligent for a senior pharmacist to do nothing about it. And why pretend she had? Unless she had something to hide? Covering up for Sister Murphy, perhaps? He shook his head. *Now you're being ridiculous,* he thought.

But at least he had an ampoule. He'd post it off tomorrow. Not to Rowan Heath—that might get back to Frances. Tomorrow morning he'd find the name of an independent lab and send it off to them.

CHAPTER THIRTY-THREE

Mr Vass died three days later during the Friday morning ward round. It was November and Jimmy shivered in his light suit as he walked from the car to the hospital entrance. Sister Murphy was waiting for him on Upper South, the ward spick and span and quiet as it always was. Eventually they came to Mr Vass. Jimmy looked at his temperature chart, noting the persistent fever.

"How do you feel?"

"Not a lot better," Mr Vass admitted.

"We've done some more blood cultures," the houseman said.

"There's no point in that." Jimmy remembered his conversation with Anthony Cosgrove. "They won't grow anything while we're flooding him with antibiotics,"

"But they have done! Strep viridans again."

Jimmy stared at him. The houseman shifted uneasily.

"The report's in the notes." He showed it to Jimmy, who glanced at it, his mind racing.

He turned to his patient and put his stethoscope to his chest. Mr Vass leant forward and began to cough. Jimmy waited for the spasm to finish, but it got worse. Pink froth appeared on his lips. He struggled for air with laboured, bubbling gasps, and froth began to billow around his mouth. He clutched Jimmy's hand, staring at him beseechingly, unable to speak. Jimmy could see the terror in his eyes as his lungs filled with fluid. He fell back on the pillow, continuing to stare as his pupils dilated and his lips turned navy blue. The rattling breathing grew shallow and then stopped. Within a minute of his first cough, he was dead.

The registrar understood that the aortic valve had ruptured and told the houseman to put out a cardiac arrest call. He watched Jimmy as Mr Vass' breathing failed, waiting for a lead from him, but he never moved.

"Shouldn't we try and resuscitate him?" he prompted.

"What?" Jimmy turned and stared, his hand held tight by his dead patient.

The registrar glanced nervously at Sister Murphy, who was pulling the curtains around the bed.

"The crash team's on its way," she said briskly. "Shall we make a start, Dr Greenhalgh?"

Jimmy brushed the pink froth away onto the pillow. He put his own lips on Mr Vass' mouth and tried to blow air into the lifeless body. The registrar looked helplessly at Sister Murphy, unable to apply cardiac massage with his consultant in the way.

She put a hand on Jimmy's arm. "They'll be here in a moment," she said quietly. "Leave him be. He's dead whatever you do."

The crash team arrived with a clatter of trolleys and loud, urgent voices. Jimmy stood up. There was a rim of pink around his mouth. He left the cubicle and walked away without a word.

Sister Murphy never saw him again.

He went straight to his office and sat behind his desk, numb with what he'd seen and the realisation of what had happened. The blood cultures could only have grown bacteria if there was no antibiotic in the blood. Mr Vass hadn't responded to penicillin because he wasn't getting any. That was why his aortic valve had rotted away; he'd been murdered.

Jimmy put his head in his hands and closed his eyes. He could see it now. It wasn't Sister Murphy at all. It was Frances. She'd fooled them all.

He opened his eyes and noticed a fax in his in-tray, dated that morning. It was from the independent laboratory, the analysis of the contents of the ampoule. He fumbled for his reading glasses, but he knew what the report would say. There was no trace of penicillin. The ampoules contained lactose, a white powder harmless when given intravenously but of no therapeutic value.

He sat at his desk for the rest of the morning, deep in thought.

Normally, he never drank alcohol during the day, but he remembered there was a bottle of whiskey in his desk, a gift from a grateful patient, and he poured a large glass. He thought of the beginning of his affair with Frances, the first time they had made love on *Felicity* anchored off Tern Island, the excitement of it, and he thought with shame of his treatment of Angela. He remembered how Frances had planted in his mind the seed of suspicion of Finoula Murphy. He thought of the enquiry, how she'd manipulated them all. And he thought of Mr Vass, drowning in his own fluid, feeling the clutch of his hand, so tight that even when he was dead, he'd had to prise the fingers open to free himself. Above all he remembered the look in his patient's eyes, pleading for his doctor to help him. *Primum non nocere,* he thought, but he had done Mr Vass the ultimate harm in his failure to stop Frances.

Jimmy refilled his glass, laid his head on the desk, and wept.

***

At 2 p.m. he left the hospital and drove unsteadily to Frances' cottage. It was locked but he had a key and let himself in through the back door.

She'd probably keep it in the kitchen, he thought. He started with the small dresser, pulling the drawers out and tipping the contents on the floor, sweeping the plates from the racks to see behind them, upending jars; nothing there. He pulled the drawers from the kitchen table and rummaged through them; nothing there. He turned to the cupboard above the sink, pulling out tins and jars of food. There were three packets of sugar in a row. The front one was almost empty and he poured the contents into the sink and tasted it—

sugar. The middle packet was unopened. He noticed that the back one was only half full, and he tipped it onto the draining board. It wasn't granulated sugar, although that's what the label said. It was a flat powder, more like flour.

"You fucking bitch," he shouted.

He continued to search, pulling out the drawer by the sink. Tea towels. In a frenzy, he hurled the drawer across the room. It smashed against the wall by the dresser, and the towels flew out. He stared at them on the floor, seeing the ampoules amongst them. He knelt down and examined one. The label said penicillin but the ampoule was open and empty. And then he saw the crimping machine where it had fallen by the wall. He picked it up and examined it, seeing how it worked, just like a big stapler.

"You fucking bitch," he repeated again and again, kneeling on the floor by the dresser in his stained and rumpled suit. "You fucking bitch."

"I'll take that," Frances said. He climbed stiffly to his feet and turned to face her. "Who else have you told?"

He was silent.

"I thought so." She smiled. "You've told nobody. You haven't the guts. Wouldn't want poor dumpy Angela to find out you've been screwing me. Shall I get the handcuffs? You can chain me to the bed? You like that, don't you, Jimmy?"

"Mr Vass is dead," he said. "You killed him."

"Yes, I know. I heard about it at work. I also found out Wendy Clarke had been nosing around the pharmacy, so I guessed you'd be here."

"You killed him."

"No! *We* killed him, *you and I*. You've known enough for a while now to work out what was going on. But you didn't want to. Couldn't bear to think what you'd been doing. Shagging a killer! Imagine what the hospital would say! You knew enough to save Mr Vass but you hadn't the guts to do it."

He hurled the crimping machine at her with all his strength. It missed her and struck the kitchen door, beside the stain made by the claret bottle three weeks before. He stared at the mark. She picked the crimper up and looked at the door, realising what he was thinking.

"Three weeks is a long time, Jimmy. Quite long enough for you to have saved him. Did he die horribly? Drowning can't be much fun, can it? I heard the fluid bubbled out of his mouth and you gave him the kiss of life. Yuk! More like the kiss of death, you spineless old fool."

He lunged across the room and she swung at him with the crimper, hitting him on the face and breaking his nose. He fell to his knees, stunned with the force of the blow. She went into the bedroom and came back with the handcuffs. She knelt beside him, swinging them in front of his face like a pendulum.

"One last time," she taunted him. "You're a rotten lover, Jimmy. Even dumpy Angela deserves better than you."

He staggered to his feet, sobbing with pain and humiliation. She watched him stumble out of the kitchen into the chill November afternoon. He followed the path through the marshes to Massingham Beach. She was right; he'd killed Mr Vass just as surely as she had. He splashed through freezing water in puddles on the beach, dazed with the blow to his head and the horror of it all. The tide was out and after some time he realised he was near the wreck. *Sirens on it, singing especially for me,* he thought, remembering his first sail with Frances. He was shaking with cold. He found a dry patch of sand and sat down beside a rusted metal railing. She found him there a few minutes later.

"We have unfinished business" she said, helping him to his feet. "What are you going to do?"

He stared at her. "What do you think I'm going to do? How many, Frances? Your husband, four meningitis patients, Mr Vass. Do you really think I could pretend none of it ever happened? What you said about Vass is true, I should have saved him: I had all the information, I knew it all, but I couldn't bear to believe I'd been screwing a monster."

She had left the cottage in a fury to follow him to the beach, unaware that she was still carrying the crimping machine and the handcuffs. She swung at him now with the crimper, hitting him hard on his left temple and stunning him. He fell to the ground with his back against the wreck, and she heaved him into a sitting position and handcuffed his right wrist to the metal, squatting beside him and slapping his face until he opened his eyes and looked at her.

"You asked how many," she said. "The six you know about and a few before." Her anger had subsided now. "It started when I was doing my pre-registration year at Parklands Hospital. I was twenty-four. I'd had boyfriends during my four-year university training but I'd never enjoyed sex with any of them. And then a consultant orthopaedic surgeon took a shine to me. We had sex often in rooms around the hospital and the pharmacy, and it was fantastic. I believed I was in love with him. I probably was. Then one day he dropped me. No explanation, out of the blue, and if I saw him after that on the wards he looked the other way. I was devastated, furious with him, and for a few weeks I never slept."

Jimmy's eyes were closed, and she shook him. "Bloody well listen. He was married with one child, a seventeen-year-old girl called Penny, and one winter evening she was admitted with meningitis. It was an interesting challenge to contaminate the penicillin, and two days after admission she died with her family beside her bed. I watched his face as he left the side room. He looked at me but he registered nothing. That night I slept really well.

"I got into it after that, not very often. I enjoyed the challenge of fiddling with the medication but I always made sure I chose patients with serious infections which could go either way. Not everybody with meningitis or pneumonia died before antibiotics, and one of my patients did live to go home. So I wasn't really sentencing them to certain death. They had a chance. All I was doing was moving the clock back fifty years, before antibiotics existed. I couldn't have done it if they didn't have a chance."

"Fuck's sake," Jimmy muttered.

She clambered stiffly to her feet, holding on to the wreck for support. "And it's the same for you. Here's the handcuffs key. I'll put it in this hole over here. I know you can't reach it, but there's always a chance that someone walking on the beach will find you and you can tell them where it is. It won't be my fault if nobody comes along." She looked around Massingham Beach. "I can't see anyone, I'm afraid, and the tide is almost here so it's not looking too good for you, but you never know, there's always a chance. I've got to rush off, Jimmy. If you do drown I hope it won't be too unpleasant, and at least you'll be able to compare notes with Mr Vass. Give him my regards."

PART FIVE:

POSTSCRIPT

CHAPTER THIRTY-FOUR

On the night she died, Finoula Murphy had written a long letter to her cousin Sean on his Connemara island. She walked with it to the postbox at the end of the road, and when she returned went straight to bed and quickly to sleep.

In her letter she told Sean when her suspicions had begun. She had felt instinctively that something was wrong about the sequence of meningitis deaths but it had never crossed her mind that they might be malicious. She took care, however, to give most of the penicillin injections herself, and it was clear to her from the enquiry that some of the members, not least the chief executive, believed that this evidence confirmed her guilt. To be banned from giving intravenous injections at this stage of her career was a humiliation from which she could never recover and for which she held Jimmy Greenhalgh entirely responsible. She had written to Sean many times since then, and her continued bitterness was expressed in some way in every letter.

However, the enquiry had planted the seed in her mind that somebody might be responsible for the deaths, and although initially she thought this ridiculous, it gradually took root. The excessive use by Upper South ward of sterile water during the period of the deaths was something she hadn't been able to explain to the enquiry but when she checked the pharmacy records and found that the ward's use of syringes had not increased, she began to feel that something was wrong. Extra sterile water must have needed extra syringes to draw it up. She had shown Geoffrey Ayling the records which a friend in the pharmacy had copied for her and which confirmed that the usual number of syringes had been supplied, nothing extra, and yet Geoffrey had done nothing about it. Perhaps he thought that it would have been a simple matter for someone to stockpile syringes from ward supplies over the months or to buy them elsewhere. Unless, of course, Upper South had never really used extra sterile water in the first place. But that would mean that Mrs Swynnerton had lied to the enquiry, and why would she have done that?

Eventually, she asked her pharmacy friend to double check supplies to the ward during the month of the deaths but was told that a decision had recently been made to keep these records for two months only, apparently to save space, and they had been destroyed. Frances Swynnerton was the senior pharmacist and must have approved this decision.

Finoula told Sean that after this she had given up wondering about the sterile water, realising there was nowhere else to go, but she could not shake off a nagging suspicion as to Frances Swynnerton's honesty.

Months later, Polly was admitted with meningitis. Finoula was a close friend of the family and had offered to wait with them in the intensive care unit overnight. She saw Frances come in at eight in the evening to open the drug trolley and apparently check the contents. Polly had seemed to improve during the night and Dr Spence was cautiously optimistic when he saw her at nine next morning, but then she went downhill rapidly and died later in the afternoon. It was as though the first doses of penicillin she had been given by the GP and in hospital were taking effect but the antibiotic thereafter was suddenly ineffective and the meningococcus overwhelmed her. This was not uncommon with meningitis and there was no doubt that Polly was very ill when she arrived at the hospital, but Finoula thought of another explanation, and her dislike of Frances Swynnerton turned into suspicion.

Of course, she told Sean in her letter, that's all it was, but a few days later it was reinforced when Matthew came to talk to her in the ward office about the missing notes. He told her that he was convinced that somebody had removed one set of notes from the pile he'd left in the library when he went for lunch. She asked him if Frances Swynnerton had been in the library, and Matthew had confirmed that she was. While they were talking, she opened the office door to check if the ward was quiet and had seen that the lid to the ward drug trolley had been left open, a major breech of security. The trolley was kept in an alcove beside the office door and above this was a window into the office, always kept open to provide ventilation. She locked the trolley with her own key. When she had finished talking to Matthew, she left the office and noticed immediately that the lid to the trolley had been left open again. She asked the staff nurse angrily for an explanation and was told that Mrs Swynnerton had spent at least an hour working at the trolley and must have left the lid open herself. Finoula realised she could have listened through the open window to every word of her conversation with Matthew and that she would have had no time to close and lock the lid when he left suddenly in a rush, having remembered he was late for an appointment.

I know none of it proves anything, she wrote to Sean, *but tomorrow I'm going to arrange a meeting with Geoffrey Ayling at his home. He'll have to see me, although I doubt if he'll want to, and I hope he won't ignore what I say. Also I admit I'm anxious for myself. She would have heard me ask Matthew if he had seen her in the library, and there was nothing in what we'd said before this to explain why I'd asked about her particularly. If she really is responsible for all these deaths, and if she thinks I am beginning to suspect her, she might come after me.*

***

Mrs Murphy was told of her daughter's death by two Garda who had driven over from Westport. Finoula's letter did not reach Inishbaron Island for a further week because a storm had prevented the *Queen of the Isles* from sailing with the mail and the newspapers. By then the Irish press had got hold of the story of the nurse who had killed patients and whose guilt was confirmed by her suicide and the discovery of the murder equipment in her house.

Sean was shattered. He saw the newspaper headlines before he opened Finoula's letter. Since their childhood, he had been closer to her than to anybody else and he believed completely that she could never intentionally harm a patient. When he read her letter and saw the date on it, he understood immediately that Frances Swynnerton must have killed her and planted the equipment in her house. A few days later, when his grief and anger were more controllable, he began to research Frances on the internet and to contact colleagues in England. After several weeks he had a plan.

CHAPTER THIRTY-FIVE

The country was short of doctors. The new ethos in hospitals, in part a consequence of management dictates and government targets, had forced senior doctors into early retirement and persuaded many juniors to emigrate. Applications for medical school had dropped off. Entry requirements were therefore less onerous, and many medical schools, including St Stephens in London, were encouraging older applicants, particularly those with a previous career allied to medicine.

On the first day of the new academic year, the dean of the medical school held his traditional drinks party for the new students. This was as much an ordeal for him as it was for them, but at least they had the consolation of free sherry. He was relieved to be approached by an attractive lady, probably in her late thirties, who seemed to have the social graces most of his new students lacked. She was quite tall with fair hair, handsome rather than pretty. It would be a few months before they slept together.

When the dean's knighthood was confirmed, he took his latest mistress to a favourite restaurant in Pimlico in celebration. He booked his usual table for two in a quiet corner well away from the entrance and the service doors. They were welcomed by the head waiter, who studied Frances with discreet interest, wondering yet again how an unattractive old man like the dean managed to get them.

Before going to their table, they sat on stools at the bar and ordered gin and tonics. The dean had installed Frances in a small apartment not far from the restaurant and they were already regular customers, usually coming on Friday nights before the dean returned to his family in Sussex for the weekend. The new barman was chatty, and Frances realised with a start that his soft Irish accent bought Sister Murphy to mind. He asked if they were celebrating and, when the dean modestly mentioned his knighthood, poured a free round of drinks.

"I love your accent," Frances said. "You must be from the west of Ireland."

"From Connemara."

"I knew a nurse from there—Finoula Murphy."

"There are lots of Finoula Murphys in Connemara," Sean said. "Where did you know her?"

"We worked in the same hospital. She was a ward sister and I was a pharmacist. She had been there for years and then she committed suicide. It seems she had been murdering patients and she killed herself because she was about to be found out."

"I think I remember reading about it," Sean said. "Was there no doubt at all of her guilt?"

"None at all. She was a psychopath."

They took their drinks to the table. Frances started with whitebait and the dean ordered oysters. They had only been together for four months but already the usual boredom was setting in. He had his eye on a very pretty dark-haired student in her second year who was at least fifteen years younger than Frances. The free Pimlico apartment was the usual clincher in a new relationship, but he had to get Frances out of it first.

She watched over her glass of Chablis as he slurped his oysters. Long silences were a feature of their relationship now. He was overweight, sweaty, with oily, thinning hair. It was time to move on and leave him to his pretty student. She had got what she wanted from him: free accommodation for a while and an unspoken guarantee that she would pass her exams. But she might as well enjoy her steak, and he always ordered an excellent claret.

She told him over coffee, "I don't want you to stay tonight, Charles. We both know it's over. I won't make a fuss. I don't expect you to find me another flat, but I'm sure you'll want to contribute to the rent when I do. I'll move out as soon as I've found somewhere and my successor can move in. She looks like a nice girl, which is a shame."

They had arrived late and were the last to leave the restaurant. She went to the bar to say goodbye to Sean, but he had already left. They collected their coats. The head waiter opened the door for them and the dean followed her out into the cold January street.

"At least let me run you back to the flat," the waiter heard him say before closing the heavy door of the restaurant. "It's a bitter night."

"Why don't you just fuck off,' Frances said.

The dean's BMW was parked only thirty yards away. He walked to it, eased his considerable bulk into the driver's seat, and closed the door. Frances rapped on the window and he wound it down.

"Don't ever come near me again. Don't rush me out of the flat— I'll tell you when I'm ready to go. Pester me in any way and I'll make sure the medical school knows about you and your taste for vulnerable students. And of course I'll have a little chat with the pretty dark-haired one. Have a nice weekend with the family."

"Bitch," he muttered, turning the ignition key as she walked off.

The explosion was heard as far away as St Stephens Hospital Medical School across the Thames.

Rory McGouran

AUTHOR PROFILE

Rory McGouran is a retired consultant physician with over forty years' experience of working in district hospitals such as St Paul's.

***

What Did You Think of *Unthinkable*?

A big thank you for purchasing this book. It means a lot that you chose this book specifically from such a wide range on offer. I do hope you enjoyed it.

Book reviews are incredibly important for an author. All feedback helps them improve their writing for future projects and for developing this edition. If you are able to spare a few minutes to post a review on Amazon, that would be much appreciated.

PUBLISHER INFORMATION

Rowanvale Books provides publishing services to independent authors, writers and poets all over the globe. We deliver a personal, honest and efficient service that allows authors to see their work published, while remaining in control of the process and retaining their creativity. By making publishing services available to authors in a cost-effective and ethical way, we at Rowanvale Books hope to ensure that the local, national and international community benefits from a steady stream of good quality literature.

For more information about us, our authors or our publications, please get in touch.

www.rowanvalebooks.com
info@rowanvalebooks.com

www.ingramcontent.com/pod-product-compliance
Lightning Source LLC
Chambersburg PA
CBHW031230260626
47169CB00007B/2227